HERE THE ROAD ENDS

JACK BENTON

ALSO BY JACK BENTON

The Slim Hardy Mystery Series

The Man by the Sea

The Clockmaker's Secret

The Games Keeper

Slow Train

The Angler's Tale

Eight Days

When the Wind Blows

The Circus Lights

Here the Road Ends

The Tokyo Lost Series

Broken

Frozen

Stolen

For Janet Hodgson

AUTHOR'S NOTE

I have taken some considerable liberty with the locations described in this book. While place names may be familiar, some places have moved, others have grown, others have disappeared.

Despite it all, I have tried to keep the indomitable spirit of Dartmoor throughout.

HERE THE ROAD ENDS

1

IT WAS TOO cold to be outside without reason, but Andy Johnson didn't seem to care. He stood with his back to the parked car, hands on his hips as he stared out across the patch of brushy moorland as though wondering what to do.

A biting wind ruffled unruly hair and tugged at the lapels of a shirt that hung loose beneath the hem of a dark green sweater. Andy slowly shook his head, then stepped forward, climbed over the leaning barrier that marked the end of the road, and started out across the moor.

In the distance, the low, rolling hills of Dartmoor shone after recent rain. A mottled green patch of forest and the distant glitter of the English Channel in a V between hills stood to the south. Half a mile away, the old St. Michael's church at Brent Tor rose on its cragged hillock, stark against the grey sky.

Private investigator John "Slim" Hardy climbed out of the ditch where he had been crouched for the last two hours. He stuffed the digital camera into his pocket with hands numb from the cold even through leather gloves, and paused a moment to shake the stiffness out of his joints. Then, after checking the zip on his coat to make sure it was right up to the neck, he climbed out onto the last section of road and headed after Andy, following the disturbance in the grass and the footprints left behind.

He remembered a time which felt so long ago now, when he had been paid to investigate another man acting in a mysterious manner, and the truth had changed his world. If he had known then the road that it would have taken him down, he might never have accepted the case, but what was done was done, he thought, as he followed an obvious trail downhill towards a stand of straggly, wind-battered trees. Andy was clearly in a hurry, stomping through bushes and leaving one deep indent in a marshy patch that could have been easily avoided. Worried now, Slim quickened his pace.

The path steepened, beginning to angle as it led down into a hollow where two hills converged. Slim saw a thicket of dead trees up ahead, caught a glimpse of Andy's jacket among the leafless boughs. He was already backing out, his business done, and Slim scrambled to get off the path before Andy turned and spotted him. He had blown his one excuse of being a fellow rambler on a previous occasion; the same explanation wouldn't wash twice.

There were few options. A cluster of low-lying rocks was the best he could do, but a crouch wasn't enough, and Slim found himself lying flat on his side, his legs curled against the rock, the sodden grass soaking through his coat into the sweater beneath.

It was enough, though. He heard Andy huffing as he climbed up the path less than ten yards away without so much as a pause. Slim lay still, counted to twenty and then got up, just in time to see Andy crest the top of the hill and vanish from sight.

By the time Slim, sodden and cold, reached the top of the path and climbed over the barrier to where the road ended, Andy's car was gone.

He waited for a few minutes in case Andy had forgotten something, then trudged down the hill to the hollow where Andy had gone.

It was starting to rain. Beginning with a gentle patter, it was growing in intensity, the grey skies threatening to downpour. Slim had already given up any hope of getting dry, so he wasn't worried about the rain's effect on him as he walked beneath the twisted boughs of several gnarled trees that appeared almost if not already dead.

A moment later he found himself standing in a muddy clearing near the riverbank of a slow, meandering stream, likely pretty on a fine day but now gloomy and grey beneath the overhanging trees. In the water, a handful of finger-length fish darted away from the shallows as Slim approached, retreating to the safety of deep water.

Animal tracks pockmarked the mud by the riverbank, those of moorland ponies and cattle, as well as dogs, perhaps foxes. They used this shallow section as a ford as well as a drinking hole, and the mud was similarly churned up on the other side.

As he had known it would be, the stone monument, a tasteful but bland stick of granite roughly the size of a postbox, was still there, tucked into the trees just back from the riverbank, its lower half green with algae and lichen, its upper half partly overgrown.

The inscription was caked with mud but still visible.

Elissa Anne Lowescroft
You flew like a bird into the sky
We watch always for your return

Slim walked around the monument, even wiping off a little dirt, but there was nothing else. No ages or dates. Only the name and the inscription, and after Andy's visit, a little blue teddy bear, no larger than the palm of Slim's hand, recently placed on the top, already sodden by the rain.

'THEY CLAIMED she suffocated in the marshy area up from the stream,' Simon Clifford, a local reporter for Cornwall and Devon Live News told Slim over a coffee in a Plymouth city centre café. 'It was one of those nightmarish scenarios that parents dread. A school trip gone wrong. They were climbing up to Brent Tor from the southwest when the weather had a turn. Fog rolled in as they headed for the coach, but Elissa somehow got left behind. Things happened quickly. A search went out that same afternoon but there was no sign of her. It wasn't until the next morning that her body was discovered.'

'You say they claimed she suffocated. In water? Why not drowned? And, who is "they", and why "claimed"?

Simon sighed. 'It was one of those grey area cases which left a lot of people, including many of us in the press, with unanswered questions. She was nine years old. She had a minor head wound consistent with having tripped and hit her head, as well as a few bruises, but nothing serious. She was supposedly knocked unconscious, allowing her to asphyxiate in the shallow water. Not an official drowning, because there was no water on her lungs, according to the autopsy report. However, the fact that she died in marshland meant that's how it was often reported and that's what many people still believe. That their was a minor head wound left many people with doubts. The parents, though, accepted it, and the police encouraged us in the press to accept it, to let the case lie out of respect for the family.'

'But of course, you didn't?'

Simon sipped his coffee. He was old now, perhaps in his seventies, but the wonder was still there in his eyes. He gave Slim a sad smile and shook his head.

'There was too much which didn't make sense. Elissa was a kid, sure, but she wasn't a baby. She rode horses in competitions. And she was a girl scout. I'm not saying she could have survived out there for days, but she wasn't stupid. Friends said she was a sensible girl, level-headed. But that wasn't all.'

Slim leaned forwards. Simon took another sip of coffee.

'There was a teacher there that day, a young guy, Philip Reece. It was his first job. He was supposed to be bringing up the rear, watching the kids. When they noticed Elissa had gone, he retraced their steps, looking for her. By the estimations of the other teachers, he was gone about half an hour, and when he returned, he was in a terrible state, babbling and incomprehensible. He had an immediate breakdown and never recovered, leaving his job and being sectioned under the Mental Health Act.'

The connotations were obvious. 'He killed her, didn't he?'

Simon Clifford smiled. 'That was the natural assumption, of course. And the police pointed the finger. But there was no evidence. And I mean, none. By all accounts he was a friendly, compassionate man who wouldn't hurt a fly. He loved his job, and he was well liked by the kids.'

'But people can flip.'

'I can tell you're a detective, John. As a reporter, I considered the same line of thought. But nothing connected Reece to Elissa's death. Nothing. Even the autopsy report, which estimated she had died a significant period of time after she had lost the group.'

'So, he blamed himself? That's understandable. What teacher wouldn't?'

'It wasn't that he had an opinion one way or another. In police interviews he was literally hysterical, screaming and wailing. I've listened to a section of the recording, and it's traumatic just to hear. I can't imagine what it was like being in the room with him. And after that, he entered a state of catatonia. Not speaking, not reacting, nothing. He was committed to an institution, where he died a few years later.'

Slim frowned. 'That sounds like an overly dramatic reaction, even to something so terrible.'

'Maybe. From the transcripts, and other reports I've read about Reece's period of incarceration, the few times doctors were able to get him to speak, he claimed to have seen something else out there in the fog that day on the moor.'

'What?'

'Another little girl. One wearing a hat. A little girl with straw-coloured hair.' Clifford, clearly uncomfortable, took a sip of his coffee and stared out of the café window. When he turned back to Slim, his cheeks had gone pale. 'No different to any other little girl, except that she had yellow eyes, and no nose or mouth.'

Slim shivered. 'It could have been a hallucination. Something brought on by stress or panic.'

Simon nodded. 'It could have been a lot of things. Unfortunately, no one ever got to ask Reece for further details.'

'How did he die?'

'He wrapped a plastic bin liner around his neck and somehow managed to strangle himself.'

Slim sat back. A ghastly end to a wretched life. As he lifted his own coffee and took a sip, however, one more question came to him, one which ordinarily might sound stupid, but now seemed of great importance.

'What colour was it? The bin liner, I mean?'

Simon gave him a grim smile. 'You're a detective, you know the way these things go. It was yellow. Of course, it was yellow.'

3

'SOMETHING MUST HAVE TRIGGERED IT,' Slim, walking side by side with Andy's mother as they headed up Exeter High Street in the direction of the cathedral. Every few steps he paused for her to catch up. She didn't like walking with a stick, she said, but Audrey Johnson had an aversion to sitting at home and insisted on taking a walk, even though an obviously dodgy hip and a stick made it troublesome.

'I mean, Andy's in his thirties,' Slim continued. 'He wasn't even born when that little girl died. And if you say there's no family connection, then there can't possibly be a logical reason for it. You say it's become a regular habit?'

'I've known about where he goes for six months,' Audrey said, 'but he's been wandering off for over a year. It took me a long time to figure out where he was going, so it's hard to know exactly when it started.'

'Do you keep a diary or anything like that?'

Audrey frowned. 'I have the one for his medicine that the doctor recommended. I could look back through it, see if there's anything in there. Some note in the margin or something. I doubt it, though. It's hard enough keeping up with him as it is. I don't have time to do such things. It's only when it became a pattern that I started looking into it. All I want to know is why.'

Andy Johnson, born 1990, thirty-three years old, diagnosed autistic, a ward of his single, widowed mother. Suffering both depression and from obsessive compulsive disorder. He was a psychiatrist's dream but a social nightmare. Still believing he had a job, his mother would help him dress each morning, take him on a thirty-minute drive around town before bringing him home again, sitting him in a spare bedroom styled as an office, where he would make marks on bits of paper, type on a computer disconnected from any networks, and make phone calls to no one.

And so it had been for the last twelve years, until Andy starting going off on "house calls", stealing his mother's car.

Once she started to realise, she had begun to track him, eventually discovering his regular attendance at Elissa Lowescroft's monument near Brent Tor, not far from St. Michael's church.

'In the end I put my phone into a pocket of his bag with a GPS tracker app running. He didn't know it was there, and when he came back, it showed where he had gone. I went out there myself to have a look. After that, whenever he disappeared, I went out there, and found he was going back to the small spot each time.'

Slim had asked it before, but now he asked it again, as always listening for any details that may have changed, any new information.

'After you stopped him using your car, he found other means?'

Audrey nodded. 'The first time, when I hid the keys, he

hot-wired it. Tell me, how does someone like him learn something like that? I didn't even know it was possible in real life.'

'It depends on the age of the car,' Slim said. 'But I agree, it's not a skill that's easy to acquire.'

'After that, I left my car at my sister's, and he used a bike.' She gave an incredulous shake of her head. 'Thirty miles. He was sick for two weeks. He nearly had to go to hospital.'

'What did you do?'

'I got rid of the bike. The next time, though, he stole Mr. Rogers's car, from number 16 across the street. It was all I could do not to have Mr. Rogers call the police. I lied and told him Andy had gone out to get his medicine, but he was furious. I'm so very lucky people round here accept Andy for what he is.'

Slim nodded in agreement. It sounded like Andy was lucky not to have been committed. It had likely happened for lesser reasons.

'And the bears? Where does he get those?'

'He makes them himself. Sews and stuffs them out of things he finds around the house.'

'I see.'

'Each one is a little different, but he uses the same basic colours. Always shades of blue.'

'He takes a new one up there every time?'

'Yes.'

'And what does he do with the old ones? Does he bring them home?'

Audrey put a hand over her mouth, stifling a sob. 'Yes. He keeps them in his room.'

'What is it?'

Audrey took a moment to compose herself. 'He keeps them in a drawer,' she said. 'And they all look so sad.'

'Could I see them? Or could you show me a picture?'

'Of course,' Audrey said. 'Oh, that poor little girl. I know he's trying to comfort her spirit or something like that, but I just don't understand why. There must be a reason. I mean, there has to be, doesn't there, Mr. Hardy?'

Slim was silent for a moment, looking down at his boots in a moment of contemplation. At last he looked up, not at Audrey, but at the sun, partially hidden behind grey clouds.

'Everything happens for a reason,' he said. 'It's just that some reasons are a little more complicated than others.'

4

DARTMOOR WAS a desolate undulation of bare hills sprinkled with bent, wiry trees, tumbling stone walls, rocky tors, patches of gorse and bracken. The best thing about the area around Brentor—the parish's name styled as a single word combined from the name of the local tor—was the tiny hilltop church, half a mile from where Elissa's monument stood by the side of a trickling stream.

Not far from the moor's western edge, where it was bordered by farmland, St. Michael's church was claimed to be the highest in England, standing at an altitude of 338m atop the rocky hill of Brent Tor. Dating from the 13th Century, the church, with a capacity of only forty parishioners, had largely had its use reduced to seasonal events, but from the outside it had spectacular views across Dartmoor and into Devon and Cornwall. South you could look right down the Tavy River valley, the English Channel visible in the distance, while to the east Dartmoor stretched away as a series of rocky hilltops.

Having parked in the little car park at the foot of Brent Tor, Slim, armed only with a packet of sandwiches and a flask of hot black coffee, walked to the hilltop and looked down on the area where Elissa Lowescroft had died.

Further to the north was the dramatic Lydford Gorge, a series of swirling whirlpools and plunging waterfalls, but the tributary of the River Burn, which ran through the valley towards Brent Tor, was altogether more sedate, in places little more than a trickle running beneath overhanging vegetation. Slim had already walked a half mile along the river in each direction from Elissa's monument, wanting to get a feel for the place, then up the hill, the ground underneath his feet dry and hard in the good weather, but filled with pits and divots which likely became soggy and uneven during rain, leaving the hillside a nightmare for unsuspecting walkers.

The nearest buildings were some distance away, Brentor village a cluster of houses over the hill to the northwest, while to the east there was nothing but a few isolated farmhouses. Many of the buildings were now holiday lets, the local population having dwindled to a few hundred, according to what internet sources he had found.

Cold calling had worked for information in the past, but the first three doors he tried in Brentor village were answered by residents who'd lived in the village less than five years and had no idea what he was talking about when he mentioned a river monument further up the valley. As he came upon the village hall, however, through the windows he noticed an older lady clearing tables from a recently finished coffee morning. He went inside, knocking on the door as he entered.

'Excuse me. I'm sorry to bother you.'

The woman, in her seventies and overweight, wearing a floral blouse that attempted to hide it, looked up and gave Slim an expectant smile. Her eyes were rheumy behind glasses, the grey in her hair fought by a weak blonde dye.

'Yes?'

'My name's John Hardy,' Slim said, at this stage of his investigation feeling no need to hide his identity. 'Are you a local? I just had a couple of questions.'

The woman put down the pile of plates she had just stacked. 'Well, I suppose so,' she said with a genial chuckle. 'Nearly twenty years now since we moved down.'

It wasn't long enough, but it was a foot in the door. 'I'm not from round here,' Slim said, coming inside and closing the door as a gust of wind threatened to tear it from his grasp. 'But I'm staying locally, and I'm interested in the history of the area. Do you think you could point me in the direction of someone who'd be able to help me?'

'Well, let me think … have you been up to Gale Farm? It's about three miles east of Brent Tor, in Willsworthy. It's still owned by William Gale. The Gales are one of the old families around here. Say it quietly, but old William is losing his marbles a little bit. They still bring him to the coffee mornings sometimes, and if you catch him on a good day, he'd probably have plenty to tell you.'

'Thanks.'

The woman introduced herself as Lilian Taylor of Brent View. Slim remembered it as one of the bigger houses just outside the village, having taken particular note of each place as he went from door to door. She explained that Gale Farm had been run by the Gale family for generations. Now, William's grandson, Aaron, ran all the day to day business, his father Jake having died relatively young and his mother moved up to London to be closer to the rest of her family, where she had later died. Aaron, in his mid-forties, now had two teenage kids in secondary school in Tavistock.

'What happened to his father?'

Lilian sighed. 'I don't know the details, but as far as I know, it was a road accident. Back in the early eighties, around this time of year, I think. He went off the road, into a tree or something. Aaron was only a boy at the time, so I heard. He was in the back of the car, but suffered only minor injuries.'

'That was lucky.'

'Yes, yes it was.' Lilian was lingering, clearly with more to say. Slim waited, letting the silence become uncomfortable, until she couldn't resist.

'Obviously it was long before we came down here, but what I do know is that it was over at Postbridge,' she said. 'It's a small village—hardly even that, really, out across the moor. It's supposed to be haunted. There have been several accidents over the years, with reports of a ghostly pair of hands pulling drivers off the road.'

5

A SMALL LOCAL bookshop in Tavistock was enough to reveal the secrets of Postbridge. With a pamphlet on Dartmoor's ghosts in hand, Slim retired to a nearby park to read, but while the story contained mention of ghostly hands twisting steering wheels and wrenching people off motorbikes on a number of occasions over the last hundred years, to Slim's disappointment there was no mention of yellow-eyed children without noses or mouths.

Nevertheless, interested in where the trail might lead, he headed out to Postbridge, which was a desolate place in the middle of Dartmoor, a cluster of isolated houses the only evidence of the village Lilian had claimed, little more than a bridge over a trickling stream. He made a couple of passes over the bridge, during which nothing untoward happened, then tried knocking on the doors of the handful of nearby houses. One was a holiday let, and he received no answer at the others.

Thinking that he'd probably come to a dead end, he drove back across the moor to Gale Farm. Parking at the end of a long, winding farm lane snaking between low stone walls and crossing a river via a stone bridge that had obviously been widened to allow the passage of modern farming equipment, he walked the rest of the way, finding himself in the shelter of farm buildings, with a smelly farmyard and a dog hassling him from a kennel outside a cow shed. He adjusted his coat, then went up to the farmhouse door and knocked.

'Just a minute!' came a voice from inside, and Slim heard the fussing of a couple more dogs. Then the door opened to reveal a blonde woman in her late thirties, rather more glamorous than Slim might have expected from such an isolated place, and looking strangely familiar. She was holding back a yapping terrier with her foot while behind her an elderly dachshund barked at the wall, apparently oblivious to Slim's presence.

'I'm sorry to bother you,' Slim said, taking a step back in case the terrier got a break and went for his ankles. 'I was looking for Aaron Gale.'

'He's out in the fields somewhere,' the woman said, finally getting the terrier under control, clipping a lead to its collar. She looped it over a coat hook set back from the door, that Slim guessed was placed for such purposes. The dachshund, losing interest, wandered back into the kitchen. 'I'm Melanie Gale, Aaron's wife. Can I help?'

She had the kind of smile you could dissolve into, and Slim wondered where he had seen her before. Perhaps describing the weather on a local news channel circa five years ago maybe.

'I'm actually looking for information on some of the local myths and legends,' Slim said. 'I heard your family is one of the oldest around here.'

Melanie laughed. The terrier gave a single gruff yap, but had otherwise calmed down. 'Some of us are. Why don't you come in? I'll call Aaron. He's probably due a cup of tea.'

She led Slim into a modern kitchen, the antithesis of the house's cottage exterior, and had him sit at a glass-topped dining table.

'I'm dragging the Gales into the twenty-first century one item of furniture at a time,' she said, giving Slim a sideways smile as she perhaps noticed his reaction, then turned away and pulled a smartphone out of her pocket. Slim, whose ancient Nokia 3310 had no signal, this time made sure to keep his reaction neutral.

Melanie went out into the hall. Slim heard the murmuring of her voice. It had a smooth, almost soothing quality, and he wondered if in fact she was a former radio host or some kind of public speaker.

'He's only in the shed across the way,' she said, coming back in. 'He'll be five minutes. Brew?'

'Coffee, if you've got it.'

'Milk and sugar?'

'Ah, black, strong, ideally brewed yesterday.'

'Got it. Will see what I can do.' As she turned away, she added, 'Was there anything in particular you wanted to know about? Sorry, I didn't catch your name.'

'I'm sorry. It's John Hardy. But most people call me—'

Melanie put down the cup she was holding with a loud crack and turned sharply. Instead of an expected frown, however, she wore a broad smile.

'Slim? Slim Hardy? No … way.'

Slim felt his brow prickle with sweat. She had that rare look of someone who knew him.

'Yes. I'm a private investigator.'

'We were watching telly the other night and they had a programme on about one of your cases.'

He forced a smile. 'I know the one.'

He had refused to participate, shunning the limelight. Unfortunately, a few people connected to the case had been willing to talk, so they had got around Slim's reluctance by using archive footage from a couple of awkward television appearances he'd done in the past, when he'd needed the money for drink.

'I can't believe you figured that out.'

'I got lucky. They glossed over that.'

'So, what are you doing here?' Melanie asked, as a loud thump indicated the opening of the front door, and the terrier, still tied up in the hall, let go with a frantic rabble of barking. The dachshund, however, had retreated to a basket by the back door and this time just lay its head on its paws. 'Are we under investigation?'

She said it with a smile while waving her hands in the air. Slim shook his head.

'Absolutely not—'

The door opened, and Aaron walked in. As Slim regarded the man, he wondered if he had been too hasty. Aaron, stocky and skin-headed, cold of eyes and sour of expression, with faded tattoos on his arms and neck, his shirt and trousers filthy and with an old scar running the length of his face from eye to chin, might not have been old enough to kill Elissa Lowescroft, but it was inconceivable that he wasn't guilty of something.

6

Aaron Gale washed his hands in the sink, then wiped them on his shirt rather than the towel hanging nearby.

'Hello,' he said, his voice deep and gruff, a rumble of the earth. The single word hinted at a strong Westcountry accent.

Slim stood up and extended a hand. 'John Hardy,' he said. 'Most people call me Slim.'

'He was on telly the other night,' Melanie said, getting another cup. 'You remember?'

She touched his arm with an unexpected level of affection, like a zookeeper with a wounded tiger.

'Yes,' Aaron said, finally taking Slim's hand and giving it a firm shake. His palm was callused, his fingers lumpy and misshapen, as though they'd been crushed in an accident.

'You're not here asking about Dad, are you?'

Although the family dynamic came off as awkward, Slim had no reason to suspect the Gales had any involvement in something that had possibly happened either before they were born or were too young to remember.

'I'm sorry about your father,' Slim said, as Aaron released his hand and sat down. He waited a few seconds, then did the same. 'But it has nothing to do with that. It's actually related to the monument for Elissa Lowescroft, over the hill on a tributary of the River Burn near Brent Tor.'

'The little girl who drowned?' Melanie said, looking at Aaron as though wanting confirmation. 'Such a terrible thing, wasn't it?'

'She was in Morton's class,' Aaron said gruffly, looking up at Melanie. 'Poor girl.'

Slim said nothing, wondering whether Elissa was being considered "poor" for her death or her involvement with this newly mentioned Morton.

'She would have been, would she?' Melanie replied. She put two cups down in front of the men, a black coffee in front of Slim and a tea in front of Aaron, who took a pack of sweetener off a tray of condiments and clicked two tablets into the cup. Slim watched the residue of the dissolving pills collecting on the surface.

'Accidental, it was ruled in the end,' Aaron said.

'Was there some speculation over the cause of death?' Slim asked.

'That what you're after?'

Slim shook his head. 'Actually, no.' Often he would keep his true intentions to himself, but he sensed honesty would be more effective with the Gales. 'My client's son has been visiting Elissa's memorial and leaving … gifts behind. He's too young to have ever known her, and suffers from a variety of mental illnesses. However, the frequency, and means with which he has kept up his … pilgrimage, have made his mother suspicious. She brought me in, but

I'm just trying to get a little background, and that led me to you.'

Aaron gave a heavy-shouldered shrug and sipped his tea.

'Place like this, there's always stories,' he said.

'Your dad used to warn you about playing up on the moor, didn't he?' Melanie said, as though Aaron found speaking for himself too much of a chore.

Aaron shot her a look of tired annoyance. Turning back to Slim, he said, 'Anywhere wild like this is dangerous. You have to respect the land.'

'This Morton,' Slim said, fearing the conversation would die if left in Aaron's hands, 'Is he a friend of yours?'

'Cousin,' Aaron said.

'Second cousin,' Melanie corrected, earning another frustrated look. 'Related to your grandfather's brother.'

'Yes,' Aaron said, sipping his tea again.

'Do you think it would be all right if I had a word with him?' Slim said. 'I'd just like to ask him a few questions. Again, I'm just trying to fill in some background. If I can just establish a link between this girl and my client's son—'

'Doubt it,' Aaron said, shaking his head. 'He's inside, isn't he?'

Slim initially misunderstood, but Melanie spoke before he had a chance to ask.

'In prison, he means,' she said. 'He's serving a life sentence.'

7

Simon Clifford was all too willing to clarify details for Slim in a Tavistock café.

'Morton Gale stabbed someone outside a bar in Plymouth,' he said. 'It must have been in the mid-nineties, although I can hunt out the exact date if you need it.'

'What happened?'

'It was some kind of revenge attack. Gang rivalry. Morton would never talk, incriminate anyone else, so his sentence was harsher than it might have been. And even though he was due to be released in 2015, a series of misdemeanours have kept him inside.'

'He sounds like a bad seed.'

Simon nodded. 'His grandfather, Roger, William Gale's brother, squandered his half of the family fortune. By Morton's time, his parents were living in a cottage on the grounds of Gale Farm, renting the property from William. Morton was a known troublemaker throughout his school years and it sadly extended into adulthood. I'm no psychiatrist, but it's not hard to see the results of an inferiority complex. His dad, Nathan, was a drinker, and his mother, Olivia, was rumoured to be having numerous affairs. Morton was one of those kids who slipped through the cracks.'

'What happened to the family?'

'Morton's father died in the early nineties, as far as I know. Cirrhosis of the liver, I believe. A typical drinker's exit.'

Slim nodded, but looked away at the same time. After nearly a year of sobriety, the tremble in his hands was barely noticeable, but it was there. Sometimes he thought it always would be, left behind as a reminder.

'I don't know what happened to his mother,' Simon continued. 'She could still be alive somewhere.'

'I can track her down if need be. Did Morton have children?'

'None that I'm aware of, but again, by all accounts he was a loose cannon, so it's not out of the question.'

'I'd be interested in talking to him, if it was possible.'

'You'd have to submit an application to the prison, since you're not family, but in the meantime, you could try writing him a letter.'

'I might,' Slim said. 'That's an interesting idea.'

He thanked Simon and left, heading for his next appointment, with Andy Johnson's doctor. Dr. Raymond Trevitt worked out of a private practice in Exeter, and had agreed to talk to Slim, but only in general terms, and only if Slim made a donation to the clinic's upkeep. Already suspicious of the doctor before he'd even entered the door, Slim found himself faced with a towering, vulture-like man who walked with an exaggerated stoop, every ceiling seemingly too low for him. Carrying a clipboard, he led Slim into a bland meeting room with a window view of a featureless lawn, and seemed relieved to be able to sit down.

'Okay, Mr. Hardy,' Dr. Trevitt said, waving a bony hand, 'fire away. What do you want to know about Andy?'

'Firstly, what is your opinion of Mrs. Audrey Johnson, Andy's mother?'

The question clearly caught Dr. Trevitt off guard. He shifted in his seat, adjusted the papers on his clipboard, and let out a little cough.

'Excuse me?'

'Mrs. Johnson has asked me to explain certain aspects of Andy's behaviour,' Slim said. 'In the vast majority of situations, when a person's behaviour abruptly changes, it's as a result of the influence of another person in their life. And the closest person to Andy is Mrs. Johnson herself.'

Dr Trevitt looked unsure how to answer. He gave a wide grimace which stretched the skin back over the bones of his face, then shook his head.

'She comes across as a very put upon but caring mother.'

Slim nodded. 'I thought the same,' he said. 'But I've been fooled before.' With a wry smile, he added: 'More than once.'

'As have I,' Trevitt said.

'Andy's father?'

'Not on the scene. He lives in Scotland, remarried. I know he contributes, though, long after Andy's care passed to the state to fund. I've seen the payments.'

'You asked the same questions?'

'When a patient first comes into my care, I do all the background checks I can. Often a condition is genetic, faulty wiring, if you like. But not always. Trauma, particularly in the early stages of childhood, can have lasting impacts. The good thing about those is that they can usually be fixed.'

'But not always?'

Trevitt gave a tired shrug. 'As doctors, we like to think so, but usually management is all that's possible.'

'And Andy's condition falls into that category?'

'Yes. But we were managing him well. This change in his behaviour appears due to external factors, as you suggest.'

'May I ask what you prescribe to control him?'

Trevitt gave Slim a pained look. 'I'm afraid that I'm pushing the doctor-patient confidentiality clause just by talking to you now. But, in general terms, we use a number of accredited medicines, as well as extensive therapy. Andy suffers from comorbidity, meaning he meets the criteria for more than one serious mental health condition, which makes his care difficult. However, I do believe Andy's situation is as well managed as such a thing could be.'

'Has Mrs. Johnson talked to you about what Andy's been doing sporadically over the last few months?'

Dr. Trevitt narrowed his eyes. 'Why don't you tell me what it is you've been told, and we'll see where our stories meet?'

It served Slim's purpose to give Dr. Trevitt a fragmented account of what Audrey had told him.

'He's been finding ways to visit a memorial on Dartmoor,' he said. 'He's been leaving gifts for the long-dead child the memorial honours. Mrs. Johnson asked me to find out why.'

'I'm surprised she hasn't mentioned it,' Dr. Trevitt said.

'Perhaps she worried that you would feel you were failing Andy, and that you would refuse to continue his treatment?'

Dr. Trevitt shrugged. 'It would fit with a person of Mrs. Johnson's standing to try to spare my feelings,' he said. 'However unnecessary.'

It could also be that she feels you responsible, Slim

didn't say. He had considered the same. It wasn't possible that Andy had found out about Elissa by chance. Slim wondered if he could have read something, but Audrey had told him that Andy struggled even with basic literacy.

No. Someone—or something—had told him.

8

TAVISTOCK PUBLIC LIBRARY had a couple of dozen books on local folklore and legends but Slim found no mention anywhere of a girl in a hat seen wandering about on Dartmoor near Brent Tor.

Slim had asked Audrey to keep an even closer eye on Andy's movements, recording every time he left the house, how long he was gone, and, if possible, where he went. While technically Andy was a ward of his mother, Audrey had never behaved like a jailer. As a result, Andy often went out alone, to the shops, the local parks, sometimes just to wander around the streets.

Slim quickly realised that short of tailing him for a long period of time, discovering the identities of his regular contacts would be a nightmare, and since Andy had committed no crime, in the eyes of the law, such behaviour could be considered harassment or stalking.

What would be easier, if time consuming, would be to discover if there was anyone who had been around at the time of Elissa's disappearance who still lived locally. If nothing else it would give him a better starting point to investigate the tragedy and Andy's possible connection.

He had tried to contact Elissa's old primary school in Rundlestone, not far from Princetown, only to find out that it had closed back in the early nineties and been converted to a private home. Kids from the area now went to school either in Princetown or nearby Tavistock, and he had had no luck trying to find where any records from the old school might now be kept.

However, in such a rural community, it was inevitable that there would be people around who had connections to the old primary school. Slim got back in touch with Lilian Taylor, deciding that if he wanted to get in with the local community, the best way might be to go for its beating heart. Forcing himself out of his comfort zone, he offered to visit a local Women's Institute meeting and give a talk on his career as a private detective.

Lilian had jumped at the chance, and just five days after making the offer, Slim found himself knocking on Lilian's door, where he was met by a white-haired, elegant woman in her seventies who identified herself as Debbie Gladstone. She led him into an opulent but comfortable living room where Lilian Taylor was pouring drinks for half a dozen other middle-aged women, all of them talking excitedly. He had driven his car to avoid the need to make an excuse if alcohol was offered, but the smell and sound of wine being poured immediately put him on edge. He was thankful to be offered a chair away from the table where a selection of tea or wine had been laid out.

He had rehearsed in his mind which parts of his investigations to discuss, and which to keep to himself. He showed them a few minor scars he had received during cases, keeping the worst hidden. And he went over a few of the more unexpected twists he had uncovered, often while glossing over the amount of sheer luck and chance that had been involved.

'It might have looked like great detective work,' he said, concluding another anecdote, 'but anyone looking for it might have seen it. It was clear from the shadow on the wall that a doorway had been plastered over. Of course, I then had to figure out a way into that room. Suddenly the worn patch in the carpet in front of the wardrobe upstairs made sense.'

The women leaned forwards. All of them, except for Debbie Gladstone, who had been rather standoffish and sat back with her glass of wine, rolling her eyes, hung on his every word. If he could ever walk away from his work, there might be a career on the after-dinner circuit.

'Weren't you scared?' asked the youngest member of the group, a blonde-bobbed woman who had introduced herself as Abigail Foster, and who had clearly drunk too much.

'Of course I was,' Slim said. 'But … you go so far, and you can't turn back. The possibility of the answer draws you more than the danger.'

'You're braver than any of us, Mr. Hardy,' said a rotund fifty-something called Brenda Abbott, whom Slim had made a mental note of because her approximate age put her firmly in the range of Elissa's potential classmates.

'I sincerely doubt that,' he said.

'Where do you usually find your cases?' Abigail asked. 'Do you take referrals?'

'Sometimes,' he said with a shrug. 'Other times the cases just seem to find me.'

'So, what exactly is it that brought you to our little

village?' Debbie said at last, staring at him over the top of her wine glass as though offering it up for a challenge. 'Are you on the trail of a local murderer?'

She held his gaze a little too long. In certain circumstances she might have aroused his curiosity, but now he felt sure it was something else. She didn't believe him; thought he was spinning them a line. Perhaps she was an amateur sleuth herself, and saw his presence as a threat to her own authority.

'Nothing of the sort,' he said, watching long enough to let her know he understood, before passing his gaze around the others. 'I was staying locally, and found myself interested in a couple of local legends.'

'Really? Which ones?' Abigail said, as everyone except Debbie craned forwards again.

'Not the Green Lady up at the vicarage?' said a lady called Dawn Stewart, with a nervous titter. She'd been picking at her nails all night, clearly uncomfortable with the evening's subject matter. 'My husband's colleague reckoned he saw her twice when he was working up there, replacing a broken drainpipe.'

'The ghost was replacing the drainpipe, or your husband's colleague?' Abigail said with a tittering laugh, receiving a few reluctant smiles at her attempted joke.

'Actually, it was out on the moor,' Slim said. 'I came across a memorial stone. One for a little girl.'

A sudden hush fell over the group. Slim knew immediately that he'd said something wrong, picked the scab of a local secret long left undisturbed. Debbie chuckled as she sipped her wine. Abigail tugged at the hem of her blouse.

'Oh, I remember you mentioning it now,' Lilian said, breaking the tension.

'I was just intrigued, that was all,' Slim said, forcing a

smile. 'It's the kind of thing that catches my attention.'

'And what have you discovered, Mr. Hardy?' Debbie asked, giving him a pointed stare. 'It was an accident, wasn't it, Brenda?'

All eyes turned to the rotund woman. 'Yes, it was' Brenda said, looking down. 'That was the conclusion of the police inquiry, at any rate.'

'I didn't mean to upset anyone,' Slim said, wishing he'd never come now. 'It was a casual interest, that's all.'

Abigail clapped her hands together, looking at Lilian for support. 'No harm done, is there?'

'Why don't we close here for the evening?' Lilian said, standing up. The others, however, didn't move. All eyes remained on Slim.

'It might have been forty years ago, but there are those of us who remember it,' Debbie said. 'It was a terrible thing.' She glanced at Brenda, who looked desperate for another glass of wine. Slim, struggling with the awkwardness of the situation, understood.

'Like I said, I didn't mean to—'

'It affected everyone around here,' Debbie interrupted 'It was an awful business.'

Slim could say nothing to dig himself out of the hole he felt he had fallen into, so stayed quiet.

'No one for coffee?' Lilian said with forced cheer, finally breaking the deadlock. Debbie huffed and got up, going out into the other room. Dawn began to collect empty wine glasses as Abigail muttered something about the toilet. Suddenly Slim found himself alone in the living room with Brenda, who still sat opposite him, her hands folded on her lap as she looked down.

'Did you know Elissa?' Slim asked quietly.

Brenda didn't look up, but gave a slow nod. 'She was my little sister,' she said.

9

HE HAD RESISTED SO LONG, but something in the way Brenda had spoken, the utter despair in her voice that his questioning had caused, triggered him. There was a pub just a short walk from the B&B where he was staying, in Two Bridges, a tiny moorland village not far from Princetown, and he found himself sitting at the bar, a pint in front of him, the end of a year of sobriety staring him in the face.

The investigation had shifted into uncharted territory, veering away from Andy in a direction he didn't want to face. It was another little girl, but this one was already too late. Elissa was dead and could never be saved.

The wounds were tearing open. A line in the sand. A crumpled letter. A mother's screaming on a voicemail that had broken his heart.

He didn't remember leaving the pub, but knew by some miracle it was before closing, because he remembered staggering out into the street with the lights glaring through the windows at his back, his shadow in front of him stretching long.

He wasn't done and knew he would find more because when he had to he always could, but some survival instinct cut in to save him. Instead of staggering up the street, looking for some closed shop or private house he could break into in search of more booze, he found himself climbing over a low stone wall, slipping down a muddy bank to a trickling river, and beginning to walk, his boots and clothes sodden, splashing up through the stream in near total darkness. More than once low-hanging tree branches raked his face, but the booze had left him numb, and he walked and walked until he could barely stay on his feet. And then, soaked and exhausted, he dragged himself out on to the bank and lay down on the damp grass.

It felt soft, comforting, the arms of a mother far better than his own.

In some ways he felt like death when he woke. His body was a mass of scratches and bruises, and his hands shook, craving more of the medicine he had deprived them of for so long, but his tolerance had fallen and the hangover was slight.

He looked around. He was lying on the grass at the bottom of a long, sloping field. The river trickled nearby, and from a little farther along the bank, a small herd of cattle watched him with disinterest.

At first he wanted more booze, but he closed his eyes, counting in his head until the feeling passed. He had lost a battle, that was all. He was still winning the war. Even so, despite the cold, he stayed there for a long time, letting nature clear his thoughts, the clean air cleanse his body.

Only when he felt like he could walk past the next pub

without the cravings taking over, did he stand up, and let life begin all over again.

Audrey Johnson could barely hide her disappointment when Slim called to tell her he was dropping the case. He gave her some spiel about finding no viable leads and not wanting to waste her money, running his mouth with excuse after excuse until he had almost convinced himself. He could hear her sobbing by the time he finally ended the call, but he just couldn't do it anymore.

Needing a drink, he packed his bags. If he was quick, he might be able to get to the car park and onto the road before the diversion to the local pub drew him. Checkout was eleven; he would be just in time for first orders, and the drowning could begin.

Or he could drive and drive and drive and hope to find his sanity somewhere along the road.

He stepped out of the B&B, hoping for a new start, not a retread of the same old one, and found Brenda Abbott sitting on a picnic table just outside the entrance.

She stood up as he stared at her.

'Mr. Hardy?' she said. 'Sorry to just show up like this. I'm afraid I did a bit of sleuthing myself.' She gave a nervous laugh. 'Lilian told me where you were staying.' She spread her hands as he continued to stare. 'I wonder if I could talk to you about my sister?'

10

HE SUGGESTED they go out to the memorial, since that was the furthest place from the booze that he could think of. Brenda drove a tatty little Corsa, slowing and hugging the hedge on every corner, her driving as cautious as her personality. They parked at the end of the unfinished road where Slim had first observed Andy, walking the rest of the way. For once, Dartmoor was still, the sky clear overhead, a light October chill standing in the air.

A little blue bear sat on top of the memorial, sagging, rain-damaged. One seam had split, and its downturned mouth made it look thoroughly miserable. Brenda sighed, picked it up in one hand, brushed the top of the monument with the other, and put the little bear into her coat pocket.

'An old school friend?' Slim said, trying to sound casual.

Brenda shrugged. 'Who knows? Sometimes I find flowers, piles of stones, even coins. I don't come up here often, but there's always something. Elissa's memorial has become something of a symbol for walkers. They leave some offering for safe travel. I'd rather it was left as a memorial for my sister, as intended.'

She sat down on a nearby rock, letting out a tired puff. Slim wished he'd had time to prepare a flask of strong coffee, but all he had was a bottle of water. He offered it to Brenda who shook her head, then pulled her own bottle out of her coat. Slim baulked at the sight of a silver hip flask and looked away until she had returned it to her pocket, thankful not to be offered, knowing that if he were, he would drink it all, every last drop.

'I'm sorry,' she said, as though reading his thoughts. 'When I come here it reminds me of all the times that we missed.' She gave a wet chuckle. 'Arguments as teenagers, planning weddings together, crying through divorces, burying our parents. Although I shouldn't say that. My mum is very much alive.'

'It must have been hard to lose a sister.'

'We were close, only two years apart. I was older, but she was the grown up one, so it hardly felt it. We could have been twins. Although, to look at us, you would never have known. She was a beanpole while I … well, I'm sure you can see. She was taller than me.' She chuckled again. 'Kind of ridiculous that she needed to die for me to catch up, isn't it?'

'I'm so very sorry for your loss,' Slim said, unsure what else was appropriate. 'Dartmoor can be wild. I suppose she was just unlucky—'

'If you believe what the autopsy report claimed,' Brenda said. 'She was murdered. Mum and me know it. I mean, the police took the easy way out. No one wanted to go digging too deep. In those conditions, an accidental death made sense, and I can see why they went with it.'

'You think they were wrong?'

'They looked at the bare facts. A nine-year-old girl goes missing on a school trip. It's foggy, raining, and we all know how easy it is to get lost on Dartmoor. She trips, hits her head, supposedly drowns in a puddle. Case closed.' Brenda shook her head. 'That babbling idiot teacher only complicated matters, but he was probably closer to the truth than anyone wanted to believe. Someone was out there that day, and that person murdered my sister.'

'What makes you think so?'

'They didn't know my sister. We grew up in Merrivale, right out on Dartmoor. The moor was practically our back garden. We were out there all the time, fishing in the streams, climbing trees, walking up the tors. And we had horses. Elissa had been solo riding for a year. She wanted to be a dressage champion. What I'm trying to say was that my sister had the Dartmoor equivalent of street smarts. Sure, one of the other village kids, one of the insular ones, they might have got lost, but not my sister.'

'No?'

'This is the bit I don't get,' Brenda said. 'The question I've never been able to answer. My sister respected the moor. In those conditions she would never, never have been left behind.'

'So what do you think happened?'

'She left the group for a reason. She turned back of her own accord, and out there in the fog, someone got her.'

11

'Don? It's Slim.' He smiled. 'Happy Halloween.'

'Slim, good to hear from you,' came the jovial voice of Donald Lane, an old friend from Slim's Armed Forces days who now ran an intelligence agency in London. 'Is it that time of year already?'

'Another couple of weeks. Just thought I'd get you in the mood.'

'What do you need from me?'

'I'm after an autopsy report. I'm afraid it's an old one, dating back to 1982.'

Don chuckled. 'My word, you like to keep me on my toes. Give me the details and I'll see what I can do.'

Slim gave Don all the details he could then hung up. Putting his phone back into his pocket, he stared out at the undulating grey-green hills of Dartmoor, wondering why the desolate place refused to let him go. He had wanted to check back into the same B&B, but its proximity to the pub had left him wary of his own self-control, so for the last two nights he had wandered aimlessly across the moors, sleeping in his car at night, subsisting on a few packets of sandwiches he had bought in a local village shop.

He was looking for something he couldn't define, but it wasn't something physical but something in his mind, an insight or revelation.

Brenda Abbott was convinced her little sister had been murdered. Her mother thought so too, and Slim had left a request with Brenda, asking to speak to her mother if the old woman agreed. After more than forty years, he doubted there was much he could do with such a cold case, and, after slipping up once, he was afraid that if he dug too deep what he might find would push him back to the booze.

He wanted to walk away, but his feet felt caught in the thick, cloying peat of Dartmoor, and it wouldn't let him go.

Audrey Johnson had called, leaving him a couple of messages, but as yet he hadn't responded. He couldn't fathom how Andy fitted into anything, and had nothing to tell her. He felt like someone had broken a jigsaw puzzle over his head and even as he scrambled for the pieces, they were sinking into the mud at his feet.

He found himself, by some chance, back at Postbridge. Clouds had rolled in but it was dry, so he crossed the old bridge a couple of times, then walked over to a flat rock and took out a flask and a sandwich.

He had only been sitting there for a few minutes, wondering how a ghostly mystery had sprung up around such a place, when he heard a rustling in the grass nearby and a little white terrier came bounding over to sniff at his leg.

'Alfie, leave the lad alone,' came a gruff voice, and Slim looked up to see a tall man in a green waxed jacket, brown trousers and a flat cap come walking over. He was in his mid-sixties or early seventies, was well-built and carried an air of authority about him. Although time had taken its toll on his hair and the sun on his skin, Slim could tell the man had been handsome in his youth, and even now carried a powerful, almost stately presence.

'He's not bothering me,' Slim said. 'He seems friendly.'

'He can be too friendly,' the man said, nudging the dog away with the toe of a wellington boot. 'If you know what I mean.'

In case he hadn't, Alfie twisted around and cocked his leg on a patch of grass before running off among some bushes, barking frantically at a pheasant which made a hasty leap into flight.

'It's a pleasant day,' Slim said.

'Sure, for this time of year. You're not local, are you?'

Slim should his head. 'No.'

'I saw you make a few crossings of that bridge,' the man said, waving a walking stick in the direction of the river.

Slim smiled. 'Someone told me a story,' he said. 'Do you live nearby?'

The man pointed with his stick again, this time at a dramatic stone house a few hundred yards back up the road, partly concealed by a stand of trees.

'Up there in Little Rock,' he said. 'My name's Brian Tate. I run the hunt kennels down in the valley there.' Another wave of the stick, followed by a smile. 'The enemy of activists everywhere.'

Slim shrugged. 'It's not something I know much about,' he said. 'I was just out for a walk. I'd heard about this place. My name's John. John Hardy.'

If the man knew him as Slim, he gave no indication. 'It's nice to meet another fan of these moors,' Brian said.

'Have you lived here long?' Slim asked. 'I mean, you must have heard the stories.'

Brian let out a dry chuckle. Alfie came running back with a stick which he dropped at Brian's feet. Brian bent and picked it up, flinging it away towards the river. The dog rushed off in pursuit.

'Of course,' Brian said. 'I've even called the police a couple of times. Never experienced anything myself, though, and I must have driven over that bridge a thousand times or more.'

'It's just a story, then?'

'The road narrows as it approaches the bridge, then there used to be a bit of a dip just before you crossed, although the council have since flattened it out. It takes people by surprise, jerks the wheel a little if you're not paying attention. Then there's another bump on the other side. Of course, this road is a shortcut across the moor, and it's relatively straight. You get a lot of people come flying through here far faster than is safe.'

'I read about a local man who died a few years back. Jake Gale?'

Brian narrowed his eyes, regarding Slim with a look of distrust which bordered on suspicion.

'That's right,' he said slowly, eyes not leaving Slim's. 'A tragic accident it was, and that's all it was.'

Slim had spoken to hundreds of people over his years as a private detective, and he could read people pretty well. Even as the little dog came running with the stick, breaking the growing tension, he knew that Brian Tate was lying.

12

Robina Lowescroft was a diminutive, spindly sparrow of a woman in her early seventies. She let Slim into a cramped, cluttered kitchen which smelled of dogs and cats with a soapy aroma over the top as though she bathed them in the stainless-steel kitchen sink.

She lived in Lamerton, a pretty valley town north of Dartmoor, in the middle of three former council houses.

'Brenda said you were a coffee man,' Robina said, moving some circulars and local notices aside to make room for two stained mugs as she waited for the kettle to boil. 'It's only the cheap stuff, I'm afraid.'

'That's fine,' Slim said.

She made two coffees, then led him to a small living room which shared many of the kitchen's same attributes: clutter everywhere, a smell of pets. A pair of mismatched but equally retro two-seater sofas were angled towards each other, a coffee table between them. A modest television occupied one corner beside an electric fire currently emanating a low heat. A fat ginger cat sat on the arm of the nearest sofa.

'He behaves,' Robina said, running one hand down the animal's back. 'I've shut the other two upstairs.'

Slim sat down. While Robina cleared some magazines off the other sofa to make room for herself, he glanced over the shelves behind the door. A few family photos, the largest faded by time of a much younger Robina, a plain but smiling man, and two little girls, one tall and confident, staring unsmiling at the camera, the other shorter and stockier, her head tilted, giving the photographer a warm smile.

Slim felt a lump in his throat. There were a few other older photos of a young Robina cradling babies, then one of the two young girls together, but from then on, the stockier girl grew up alone, becoming a spotty but still smiling teenager, a young mother of her own, then finally, in the newest photograph on the mantelpiece over the fire, a middle-aged woman with two older teenage boys.

'Elissa looks like a strong-minded girl,' Slim said, unsure how else to break the ice.

Robina sighed as she lowered herself into her seat, her joints creaking. The cat immediately shifted from its position to take up residence on her lap. It did a couple of circuits before slumping down, its green slitted eyes watching Slim with the wariness of a bodyguard.

'She never was one to smile for a photograph,' Robina said. 'Yet she was such a happy girl, very kind to everyone. She loved animals, too, even cats, despite having an allergy. She could be a little taciturn sometimes, as though she were born at the age of forty and resented being a child. I never did that grieving mother thing and keep her room intact, because she had so few toys or anything like that. And Brenda ended up growing into many of her clothes. I just kept a box of a few things, a few school books. And my pictures, of course. It never really goes away, though. I can remember it as though it were yesterday.' Robina shivered despite the heat. 'That uncomfortable feeling when you hear the school bus pull away and you wait for the door to go, but it never does. And then the phone rings, and before you even pick it up you know it's going to be bad, and it is. It's the worst news in the world.'

Slim closed his eyes. 'I can't begin to understand your loss,' he said.

'You don't have children of your own?'

Slim looked at her and forced himself to smile. 'I'm afraid it passed me by,' he said. 'Once....' He shook his head. 'It didn't work out,' he said slowly, forcing a note of calm into his voice, wondering whether it was better to have known your child and lost them, or to have never know them at all.

'If I hadn't seen her body for myself, I don't think I could ever have let go,' Robina said. 'I can understand how these parents of these kids who go missing must feel. If I hadn't seen her poor little body, I would still be waiting for her to come home to this day.'

'At least you have some closure.'

'Some,' Robina said. 'Not enough. I've never been given a suitable explanation for what happened. So much about her actions that day don't make any sense.'

'Tell me what the police told you, if you don't mind.'

Robina sighed. She gave the cat a comforting stroke.

'If you ask me, it's all a little too blasé. The school party went out to the moor as planned, and everything was going fine until the walk back to the coach. The weather turned unexpectedly, as it tends to do up there, and a fog rolled in. George Stockwood, the headmaster, decided they needed to hurry, but Margaret Leddon, the class teacher, didn't want the kids to leave behind the objects they'd been collecting for a class project. Therefore, several of the kids were laden down with bags of twigs and stones.'

'You'd think they would have left them.'

'There was an ongoing power struggle between those two teachers,' Robina said. 'It was well-known at the time. Mr. Stockwood quit that same year and moved back up country. Ms. Leddon had been eyeing his job for years but when the news reported that the reason Elissa had gone back was because she had forgotten her bag, she was forced to quit, too.'

'Do you know what happened to Mrs. Leddon?'

Robina shook her head. 'Sorry, I have no idea.' Then, with a dry chuckle, she added, 'And it wasn't Mrs., it was always *Ms.* She wasn't married that anyone knew of, except to the job, and got angry if the kids got it wrong, so Elissa said. As for Mr. Stockwood, I heard he died, though. That must have been twenty years ago now.'

'Was it true? About the bag?'

Robina shook her head. 'No. She had passed it to a classmate. There's one reason she might have gone back, though.'

'What?'

'We didn't find out for years, but in 1985, a hiker found an old rusting knife out on the moor, not far from where the group had lunch. Around that time, a couple of people had been robbed up in the car park there, and the police thought it might have been connected to that. However, it had been out there a lot longer. I got a phone call one day, and the police showed up with the knife. It was in pretty bad condition but was identical to one I hadn't seen since the day Elissa went missing. She must have taken it up to the moor with her.'

'Why would she do that?'

'I put an apple in her lunchbox. She liked them cut,

but I hadn't had time that morning. That's all I can think of. The police thought it might have been to cut pieces of bracken, but there's no way. Elissa was a bit of a tomboy. We'd got her a penknife for her most recent birthday. They found that in her bag, even though children had been instructed not to carry anything like that with them. She was a very practical girl, and carried it with her everywhere.'

'Couldn't she have cut the apple with the penknife?'

Robina nodded. 'Of course.'

'So why the need for a larger kitchen knife?'

Robina shivered again. 'I don't know. The only other thing I've ever thought is that she might have been scared about something. But if she was, why on earth did she leave the group?'

13

Simon Clifford gave a sage nod when Slim mentioned the knife.

'It was found so long after that it didn't really cause many waves,' he said. 'After all, Elissa's cause of death was asphyxiation. She had a few bruises, but no injuries consistent with a knife. Plus, it was her knife. She had taken it up there that day, for reasons that are unclear.'

'She could have worried that her mother would be upset.'

'It's possible.'

'Yet everyone tells me she was a sensible girl, who understood the dangers of the moor.'

'Allegedly she was.'

'So why go back?'

'You tell me, Slim. You're the detective.'

Slim sipped his coffee. 'Because she wasn't in any danger. She didn't consider the conditions to be dangerous, so she went back of her own accord.'

'Again, it seems likely. However, that's not the narrative

that the police wanted to entertain at the time. They were very much for the "little girl lost" theory.'

'But you told me before that she wasn't found until the following day. How large was the search that went out for her? Could they have missed her?'

'It's entirely possible. However, by that evening the fog had cleared. I believe there were roughly twenty-five police officers along with a couple of dozen locals. They could have missed her. And the autopsy report contained an analysis of the contents of her stomach. The state of digestion of her lunch suggested she had died roughly six hours after going missing, after nightfall, while the search was in full swing. And she was found only a couple of hundred yards from where she was last seen. As I say, she could have been missed, of course. But it's highly unlikely.'

'So, the assumption is that she wandered off across Dartmoor, out of range of the search party, then died sometime after dark, having somehow wandered back to where she had started, avoiding the search party along the way?'

'Something like that, yes.'

'And that theory was just accepted?'

'After the cause of death was determined as accidental, there was no reason to doubt it.'

'Only the obvious overlooked possibilities,' Slim said. 'We're assuming this was a girl with the brains to understand what danger she was in. This is also a girl who left a kitchen knife up on the moor.'

'Another thing. A police officer I interviewed off the record some years later claimed the knife had been hidden.'

'Hidden?'

'It was found lodged into a crack on a flat piece of rock

below the tor, a rock popular with picnickers. A place where it would be easy to find again.'

'So she could have hidden it intentionally with the plan to retrieve it later?'

'Yes.'

'What would have been the reason behind such a thing?'

Clifford shrugged. 'I always believed she'd hidden it during lunch to stop her teacher seeing it. She would have been in big trouble if it had been seen. She could have been suspended from school.'

Slim stared into his coffee and shook his head. 'No, that's not it. If she had that kind of concern, she wouldn't have taken it in the first place.'

'Then what?'

A possibility Slim didn't even like to consider had come bubbling to the surface. He shook his head again. 'I'm not sure.'

'It's a conundrum,' Clifford said.

'Sometimes the simplest answer is the one to look for,' Slim said.

'I don't have any simple answers,' Clifford said. 'It's baffled me for decades.'

Slim gave a slow nod, then stood up. 'I need to make a phone call,' he said.

14

IT WAS uncomfortable to sleep in his car, but Slim still didn't trust himself around any kind of civilisation.

A couple of days after talking with Simon Clifford, he found himself out on Brent Tor, standing halfway up the hill, looking down on the shallow valley where Elissa Lowescroft had died.

Before he had carelessly let his phone battery run out, he had heard back from Don. He was still working on getting hold of the autopsy report, but he had come up with some other information.

A class photo from 1982, taken at the beginning of the new school year, just a couple of weeks before the fateful school trip. Twelve pupils, the main teacher, Margaret Leddon, and the class assistant teacher, Philip Reece. Leddon, sitting in the middle, had a chin-up, hard-nosed look about her. Reece, standing on the left, wore a wide, almost childlike grin.

Don had managed to put names to nine of the children, among them Elissa Lowescroft, standing just behind Margaret Leddon, and Morton Gale, sitting at the far right with a bored look as he stared past the camera at something more interesting.

Don had done his best to trace those he had managed to name. Two were already dead, one from an unfortunate accident, another from cancer. Two others lived overseas, and one in Scotland.

Two of the other three named pupils lived upcountry, and Slim had sent messages to the contact emails Don had found. It felt as though what had happened that afternoon on Dartmoor had left the children traumatised to the extent that they had left the area as soon as they could and had never come back. Slim was confident that if he could get just one of them to speak to him, he would be able to identify the other three. He hoped to speak to all of the living pupils in time, but in the meantime, Don had managed to find one good lead.

Another of the children in the photograph was Ginny Tate, daughter of Brian, the man Slim had met at Postbridge a few days ago.

Ginny had no online presence and Don could come up with nothing other than her name, leaving Slim no choice but to visit the old man again. Their first meeting had been terse, and Slim doubted Brian would be pleased to see him, but frosty receptions were something to which he had long grown accustomed.

He walked across the moor to Postbridge, armed only with a couple of bottles of drink and a sandwich he had bought in a village shop. At Postbridge, he sat down beside the old bridge to wait. Hoping Brian might spot him from the window of his house and wander down, however, proved a waste of time. Soon it began to get dark. Slim, several miles from his car as the crow flew, or at least double by the safer road, began to wish he'd just driven over in the first place. As a light blinked on in Brian's upstairs window, however, he figured he might as well go and knock.

From the bridge, only one corner of the house was visible behind a screen of trees, but as Slim walked up the road in the gloom, it came into view, set in its own spacious garden, mostly lawns of hardy moorland grass with a few stone flowerbeds along the edges. A path paved with slate led up to the front door.

Slim paused at the garden gate and looked up. The only window light that was on was upstairs. He couldn't see Brian inside, so he headed up the path and pressed a doorbell haphazardly fitted to the stonework beside the door.

A muffled buzz came from inside. No dog barked at the sound, so perhaps Brian was out. Maybe he was married, and his wife had turned on the upstairs light. Slim couldn't recall whether Brian had said, but a moment later the door handle creaked and the door opened a few inches, stopped by a security chain.

A woman's face peered out of the gap. About Slim's age, she was thin and mousy, brown eyes, ponytailed hair flecked with grey streaks. Slim immediately dismissed this woman as Brian's wife, purely because of the physical resemblance. She was thin where he was thick and stout, but she had the same eyes, the same nose.

'I'm sorry to bother you,' he said. Then, taking a chance, he added, 'I was looking for your father.'

The woman shrank back just a little. 'He's not here,' she said. Then, perhaps aware of what she was saying to a stranger at her door in the middle of nowhere, she said, 'He'll be back any minute.'

'Thanks,' Slim said. He took a step backwards, making to turn away. 'Could you tell him John Hardy stopped by? We met the other day, out on the moor.'

'Sure, I'll let him know.'

Slim took another step back. 'You're not Ginny, by any chance? Brian's daughter?'

'It's Ginette, these days,' she said. 'Yes, I am.'

'Oh, right.' Slim looked down, feigning confusion.

'What is it?'

'Oh, nothing,' Slim said. 'I couldn't possibly—'

'What?'

He grimaced, trying to appear as though he were wrestling with his conscience. It wasn't hard; in many respects he was. Every morning, when he woke up in his car, he was tempted to just head for the A30 and leave this place behind, but as so often happened, the mystery had caught him in its net, and he had only two choices now. Swim, or drown.

'It's just … I'm something of a local history buff. I've been looking into local history and was reading up about the little girl whose memorial is over the moor by Brent Tor. Elissa Lowescroft?'

Ginny shifted. 'What about her?'

'Weren't you in the same class? Do you remember much about that day?'

Ginny gave a frantic shake of her head. 'I didn't hardly know her,' she said. 'I don't remember anything.'

And with that, she slammed the door in his face.

15

Sooner or later Slim had to renter the world, so he booked back into the same B&B in Two Bridges. He had been sleeping in his car for five days, for most of which time his phone had been switched off, but now as he finally charged it again, he found several missed calls and voicemails. Loading his laptop for the first time in as long also brought him a couple of dozen emails. Most were junk, but one was from the prison authority.

His request to visit Morton Gale had been granted.

There was also a missed call from Don, so sat up in his room beside a coffee machine the landlady had lent him, Slim called his friend back.

'Don? It's Slim. Sorry, I went off the grid for a while.'

'Ha, I figured as much. Listen, I managed to get hold of one of those missing kids. Her name's Victoria Aldridge. She lives in Somerset now but she said she'd be happy to speak to you about what happened that day. She told me she'd only been at the school for a few months and after the events of that day, her parents moved her to a different school.'

'That's great, Don, thanks.'

'I'll email over her contact details.'

'Thanks, Don. By the way, I found Ginny Tate. She lives with her father. I'd really appreciate anything you can find out about their family.'

'I'll have a look and get back to you.'

'Thanks.'

Slim hung up. Buoyed by what he had learned, he pulled out a sheet of paper and began to jot down a few notes. As he did so, however, he remembered the reason he had come here in the first place.

Andy Johnson's strange behaviour. While he felt like he was starting to uncover a few fossils related to Elissa Lowescroft's death, he had found nothing at all to connect her to Andy.

Something was compelling him to leave the little bears on her memorial.

What was it?

Or whom?

Slim sent an email to Victoria Aldridge, introducing himself and suggesting a convenient time for a meeting. Then he sent a response to the message from the prison authority, doing the same.

Sitting back on his bed with a cup of coffee in hand, he wondered if he was doing the right thing. On the one hand, Elissa was already dead. He couldn't hurt her any more. On the other, there was plenty of trauma he could cause to her community, if he dug too deep.

Then he thought both of Robina Lowescroft, who still doubted the police conclusion about her daughter's death, and Audrey Johnson, who had devoted her life to her son's care.

Two mothers, both struggling with their own kind of trauma. He rarely thought of his own long-dead mother, who had been a ghost even when she was around, rarely bothering with him. She had kept him clothed and fed enough to survive, but her attention ended there.

Both Robina and Audrey deserved answers, didn't they? And if he had the means to find them, surely he would be doing some good?

It was getting late, but he couldn't sleep. He went downstairs, informed the landlady that he was going out for a walk, then headed out into the night.

The local pub, he was relieved to see, was closed, so he walked out of the village, past the last of the streetlights, and out along moonlit roads, hemmed in on both sides by tall hedgerows. The kernels of acorns crunched underfoot as the land slowly rose, until he found himself stopping at a farm gate which looked out across a flat valley of farmland towards Dartmoor.

Silhouetted against the clear night sky, the tiny St. Michael's church stood proud and tall atop its hillock, a jarring rectangle, unnatural among the flatter, rounder tors further out across the moor.

It both unnerved and impressed Slim. Not a man enamoured by the trappings of religion, from pictures he had seen it looked cramped and gloomy inside, leaving little positive impression on him. The views from outside were spectacular, however, and it would prove useful as a refuge from a storm.

He frowned. The church was less than a mile from where Elissa had died, far for someone unfamiliar to the area, but for someone local, someone who spent their free time around this corner of the moor, it was a fairly easy walk.

Had Elissa avoided the search party by hiding inside the church, later venturing outside, where she had been met with an accident?

Or had someone else, already taking shelter from the fog, encountered the girl?

Slim's mind whirled with ideas. He looked at the church a moment longer, until a cloud drifted across in front of the moon and shrouded the moor in a veil of darkness.

Slim had his coat, but shivered anyway as a breeze rustled the nearby hedgerow. He turned, waiting for the moon to reappear, then headed back towards the village, his thoughts churning, wondering whether he would be able to sleep tonight.

16

SLIM PREFERRED to meet in person, but Victoria Aldridge lived too far away to visit, so he arranged his laptop on the bedroom's desk, made sure his coffee was ready, and set up a video call.

Victoria was an affable woman, still attractive at fifty. Slim, of a similar age, couldn't help finding himself drawn to her bubbly personality. Even though he had made the reason for his call clear, she talked for a few minutes about life in general, waxing lyrical about the state of the country and the sheltered nature of today's youth, neither of which Slim, who never watched television, rarely read newspapers, and outside of cases interacted with as few people as possible, knew much about.

'So, it's Slim, is it? That's an almost classic nickname. Why on earth do people call you that? Did you ... ah ... lose some weight?'

He smiled at her directness. 'Nothing like that. I'm afraid it's not an interesting story.'

'Go on, tell me. We might as well get to know each other. Everyone at school called me Alice because I was always falling asleep at the back of the class, and believed every conspiracy going.'

Slim shifted uncomfortably. 'Well, I was in the first Gulf War.'

'Really? You don't look that old.'

'Thanks … I think. I was eighteen. It was my first and only deployment.'

'Wow, I bet you have some stories to tell.'

'Ah, one or two. But, anyway, there were four of us, and we were tasked with moving a—'

Victoria put a hand across the screen. 'Hang on a minute. The cat wants to go out.'

She got up, leaving Slim staring at a section of floral wallpaper. He heard a door open and close, then Victoria reappeared, settling back into position.

'Anyway,' Slim said, taking the opportunity to change the subject, 'I'm researching the death of Elissa Lowescroft on Dartmoor in October 1982. I heard that you were there that day? Thank you for giving me your time, and if at any point you feel upset or uncomfortable, please let me know.'

'Oh, mists of time and all that. We weren't really friends. I'd only been at that school a couple of months and hadn't really settled in. I didn't like her, if I'm honest with you.'

'You didn't?'

'Don't get me wrong, we were only kids, but you know how these things are. You go on first impressions, and at that age it only takes one word to shape an opinion, you know?'

Slim smiled. 'I know.'

'I mean, it's hard to recall anything specific, but half of the kids at that school, they were stuck up gentry types. Into showjumping, climbing trees, and hunting, and I'm this little slip of a girl from the city who's a vegetarian—

thanks, Mum—years before it's even a common thing, and I just didn't fit from the get go. Mum had moved us from Birmingham because she wanted this eco, plant-based life, and instead we found ourselves surrounded by hunt enthusiasts who had hog roasts on Saturdays. Mum felt like we'd entered some otherworldly cult, and we were gone again soon after what happened to Elissa. Her death sped the process up but it was going to happen anyway.'

'What do you remember about the events of that day?'

'I was still the new kid, and I'd only been up on the moor a couple of times. The only girl I was friendly with was absent that day so I remember being pretty lonely, just kind of wandering about collecting stones and leaves.' She smiled. 'Mr. Philip was giving me plenty of attention because I was on my own, trying to stop me feeling left out.'

'Mr. Philip?'

'Yeah, Philip Reece, his name was. He was an assistant teacher, but he was basically just a classroom helper, because he was newly qualified, I think. He kind of stood out because he was a young guy when most classroom helper types were old women. He was always friendly. He told everyone to call him Mr. Philip, and most kids did. Only Elissa and her group didn't. They called him Mr. Reece to his face and Reedy Reece behind his back.'

'Why?'

'Oh, he had one of those whiny kind of voices. A bit annoying really. But like I say, he was nice to me, and when most people weren't, I really appreciated it.'

Slim had one or two suspicions about the young assistant teacher, but for now kept them to himself. 'What do you remember about the moment Elissa disappeared?'

'It was strange. There was a bit of a sense of panic as we headed down to the car park, because the fog had come in so quickly. Some of the local kids who lived by the moor were totally unconcerned, as was Ms. Leddon, our class teacher. It was more a frustration than a concern, if you get my meaning. She was snapping at us as we were coming down, and Morton had hit someone with a stick so she was angry about that.'

'Morton?'

'Morton Gale. I suppose he was the class dropout if you like. The clown and the thug rolled into one. Barry Davis had knocked over his lunchbox up on the tor, and we'd all heard Morton promise payback. He hit Barry with a stick, and it was as Barry started crying that someone called out that Elissa was missing.'

'And Philip Reece volunteered to go back for her?'

Victoria shook her head. 'Oh no. Ms. Leddon was going to go, but old Stockwood had turned his ankle on the way down, and she couldn't really leave Barry on his own. She told Mr. Philip to just walk down to the river and holler for her, for Elissa, but I suppose he must have gone down there and when he didn't find her, he decided to go back up towards the tor. And then he must have seen what he thought he'd seen, because we all heard him screaming.'

17

'So, at first there was no sense of panic?' Slim said, leaning forwards over the laptop screen.

'Not until Mr. Philip starting screaming like he did. I remember Ms. Leddon being angry that Elissa had gone off. She didn't like the girl much, I know that for a fact. I'd heard her shouting at Elissa a couple of times. Like, proper hollering. Teachers can't get away with that these days, but back then they'd bawl you out for the tiniest of things, and Elissa seemed to get it from Ms. Leddon as often as anyone.'

'Do you remember what for?'

'Backtalk, that kind of thing. Elissa had a gob on her. I imagine, if she hadn't ... I mean, sooner or later it would have got her into trouble. But Ms. Leddon, she was an old-school dragon. Rarely a day went past without someone getting it.'

'What about the headmaster, Mr. Stockwood?'

'I don't remember him much. He was kind of taciturn, but harmless. Didn't smile all that often, never looked happy. That's why everyone liked Mr. Philip. He was basically a teacher but a kid at the same time.'

'How did the other two teachers treat him?'

On the laptop screen, Victoria shrugged. 'Okay, I suppose. They were just teachers, you know. We didn't pay them much attention unless they had an argument about something.'

'And did they? What happened when Reece came back?'

Victoria whistled through her teeth. 'Oh, gosh, I remember that bit. He was literally wailing, like hysterical screaming. We were waiting at the top of the slope down into the valley. He came running up the hill out of the fog and would have run straight through us if Stockwood hadn't stepped into his way, literally knocking him over. I remember at first thinking it was a joke, like a wind up? I thought, "Ah, in a sec he'll look up and grin and Leddon will go mental", but he just went on and on, thrashing about, screaming that he'd seen something down in the fog by the river. We were getting a little upset by that point, which is when Stockwood decided to take the kids back to the coach and leave Ms. Leddon to deal with Mr. Philip.'

'So, you went back to the coach?'

'Yes. Stockwood made us all get on the coach and wait. It was awful. A couple of kids were crying. Morton was being a clown, telling people Elissa was dead.'

'Why would be say that?'

'He was just trying to wind up some of the weepier girls.' Victoria rolled her eyes. 'And it was really working. I have no idea what might have happened when he found out the truth. That was literally the last time I ever saw him. School was closed for a week and then Mum pulled me out.'

'What happened after that?'

'Stockwood asked the coach driver to go to a payphone down the road to call the police, because his ankle was hurting, I suppose. Then he waited outside for Ms. Leddon and Mr. Philip. I remember hearing a thump like he had kicked the side of the coach, and figured he must have been really mad to do that with a bad ankle. On the coach, though, we were left to our own devices. It was way too big for our small group, and kids were running up and down, causing havoc.'

'How long were they gone? Do you remember?'

Victoria gave another shrug. 'Oh, less than half an hour, maybe twenty minutes? Not that long, but long enough. Mr. Philip still hadn't calmed down when they appeared, Ms. Leddon literally dragging him. I remember he lay down on the ground outside while Ms. Leddon talked with Stockwood. He was still laying there when the police arrived. They thought it was all about him and wasted a bunch of time. They were standing around for ages before anyone actually went back up to the moor. Then, when a second police car arrived, I suppose they took over. Mr. Philip was helped into the back of a police car. Ms. Leddon stayed up there, but Stockwood got back on the coach and we returned to the school. That was the last I had to do with it.'

Slim gave a slow nod. 'Thank you very much for your time,' he said.

18

'Twenty minutes,' Slim said to Simon Clifford, sitting across from him in the same Tavistock café where they had met before. 'It sounds like nothing, but it makes both of them suspects.'

'Margaret Leddon and Philip Reece?'

'I have a witness who states they stayed behind, and states the period of time to have been about twenty minutes.'

'You have to remember that it was a long time ago and that Victoria Aldridge's memory might not be what it was.'

'I've considered that. If I can find other witnesses to corroborate, I'll have a more accurate idea. What I'd very much like to know is what happened during those minutes where Margaret Leddon and Philip Reece were alone after Elissa went missing.'

'Leddon gave a witness statement to police,' Clifford said. 'I have a copy somewhere. I remember she said that she was hindered in any attempt to locate Elissa by Philip Reece's "sudden dramatic turn". She gave the period of time as about five minutes before they walked down, and said that when it was clear she had to take Reece down to the coach, she planned to go back for Elissa, but it was the headmaster, Stockwood, who suggested they wait for police.'

'She blamed him?'

'Not directly but the tone was obvious. Stockwood, in his statement, claimed that Elissa's upbringing, personality, and knowledge of the moor meant he chose to wait rather than undertake a search. None of them were local. Leddon and Philip Reece were from upcountry, and Stockwood was from Exeter. They'd been up on the moor before, of course, but none of them had intimate knowledge of it. He believed that by going back he would be putting more people at risk.'

'So effectively he saved himself.'

'He claimed his priority was the safety of the other children, but when those words got out in the local newspaper, it didn't go down well. He was forced to resign.'

'You say "got out in the local press"? Would you have been involved with that?'

Clifford looked down. He stirred his coffee for a moment before looking back up.

'I had a niece of Elissa's age at school in Tavistock at the time,' he said quietly. 'There was a lot of anger in the community and people wanted a scapegoat. My piece was … unfavourable, critical, even. Unfairly so, looking back on it. Of the three teachers there that day, Stockwood is the only one who can be conclusively ruled out of any wrongdoing. Negligence, maybe, because perhaps he could have anticipated the weather better, but otherwise he just got unlucky.'

'And you condemned him for it?'

Clifford grimaced. 'I wasn't alone, but I certainly added a little fuel to the fire. When there's a tragedy like that, people find it hard to just shrug and move on. They need somewhere to direct their anger. Stockwood was the obvious choice.'

Whether he agreed or not, on a certain level Slim understood. He had been that man.

Clifford had another appointment, so after he left, Slim wandered around Tavistock, taking some comfort in the bustle of the little valley town. He had reached that stage of the investigation where his mind was whirring with ideas but refusing to put them into any kind of order.

He was thinking of going back to the B&B when his phone rang. To his surprise, it was Brenda Abbott, Elissa's sister.

'Hello, Slim?'

'Brenda. How are you?'

'You know, not too bad. Are you still around? I was going through the loft, and I came across some boxes of Elissa's things. Mum didn't have room for them, so I stored them away years ago. It looks like mostly junk, but if you want to have a look, you're most welcome.'

Slim nodded. 'I very much would,' he said. 'Are you at home?'

'Yes.'

'Then I'll come over right away.'

19

THEY SAID one man's junk was another's gold, but the same distinction worked the opposite way. A dozen or more junior showjumping trophies were of little interest to Slim, even though Brenda, cheeks glowing with pride, seemed insistent on explaining the circumstances regarding each and every one.

'She was behind on the last jump for this one,' Brenda said. 'It was a three-pointer, and none of the other girls had got over without clipping it. Elissa took it a foot earlier than the rest and Pinkie sailed it. We were so proud.'

'That's nice,' Slim said, trying to maintain interest amidst a sea of unfamiliar terminology. He assumed Pinkie was a horse. 'I gather she was good, then.'

'Best in Devon in her age group,' Brenda said. 'Mum hoped she might ride in the Olympics one day. She'd have had to go to an equestrian college or something, but I know Mum was already putting money away.'

As Brenda reached for another trophy, Slim pointed to a pile of old school books, hoping to distract her. 'What are these?'

'Oh, just some school exercise books,' Brenda said, confirming Slim's suspicion. 'Mum probably never got around to throwing them away.' She held up a handful of tatty exercise books and thumbed the pages, giving Slim a quick glance at pages of squared paper covered in handwritten, rudimentary sums.

'See,' Brenda said. 'These are mostly maths, I think. I don't know why anyone would keep these.'

She put them behind her as though planning to throw them away, but Slim put out a hand. 'Could I have a look at them?'

'If you really want.'

'Something written by Elissa herself might give me an idea of her personality.' He smiled, remembering something an old friend had said. 'You'd be amazed what handwriting can show about a person.'

She handed them over to Slim, who flicked through them quickly as though trying to give the impression he knew what he was looking for. Brenda was watching him expectantly, and he felt a sudden pang of embarrassment, like a quack doctor prescribing a pill made of chalk and claiming it would cure all ills. It was obvious from the rows of sums that there was nothing useful in these books, but if he returned them so soon Brenda would think him a fraud.

'Can I borrow these for a few days?' he asked. 'I'll take care of them.'

'Sure. I wish Mum had kept more, but I think she had to throw away a lot of Elissa's things a few years ago, when they moved.'

'It's hard to keep everything,' Slim said. 'Even when you're trying to hold on to someone.'

After leaving Brenda's place, he drove back to Two Bridges and returned to his B&B. He put the bag containing the old exercise books on the desk and made coffee. Then, sitting on the edge of the bed, he called Don.

'Any news on those last couple of names?' he asked. He had asked Victoria, but she had struggled to recall the names of more than half the class. He wanted to visit Ginny Tate again, but felt a little reluctant after the frosty reception last time.

'Still trawling,' Don said. 'I'll haul something up in the end. Just give me a little time. Anything else you need?'

'I'd like to talk to someone associated with any of the teachers there on that day,' Slim said. 'If you could have a look for me, that would be great.'

He hung up. It was dark outside now, a little after eight o'clock. Slim's stomach was grumbling and he had nothing to eat. The B&B didn't serve evening meals so he went outside. There was still time to find a local supermarket or a petrol station shop somewhere, but Slim had spent a lot of the day in the car and didn't feel like driving again.

At the end of the street, the lights of the local pub called to him.

I can handle it. If I stay in the family room, or the restaurant section. I don't need to drink.

It was a massive risk after his previous relapse, but Slim had never been one to resist holding his fingers to an open flame. He walked up the road to the pub, took a deep breath, and went inside.

The smells and the sounds were like the welcoming arms of an old friend. It was a typical country pub, low ceilings, cozy, seemingly as much bar as seating space. Worn spots in the carpet. Faded photos of local sports teams. A pile of old magazines on a shelf inside the door, most to do with horses, hill walking, or game hunting.

There were few customers, just a pair of old men talking at a table in the corner, a younger couple eating dinner at a table through a side door, near a huge log fire that was crackling gently. Slim walked up to the bar, surveyed another line of old friends, and was about to select the first of too many when a woman appeared through a backroom entrance and leaned over the bar.

Slim blinked in surprise as he recognised Melanie Gale.

She smiled sweetly at him, an incongruous beauty in this wild place, where most of the people Slim had seen looked as weathered as the tors. He was so surprised that at first he said nothing, just met her gaze until she tilted her head and frowned.

'Well, well, John "Slim" Hardy. What a surprise to see you in here.'

'Melanie Gale,' Slim said 'It's a surprise to see you too.'

She shrugged. 'Subsidies aren't what they used to be. The money helps. How has your investigating been going? What can I get you?'

The decisive moment. Melanie knew nothing about him, but under her gaze Slim couldn't bring himself to reveal his worst version.

'Do you still do coffee at this time of night?'

Her eyebrow rose again. 'You don't like to sleep?'

'Actually, I don't like to drink. I was hoping I wasn't too late for food.'

'I see.' Melanie glanced at a wall clock near the door. 'You still have time. Why don't you find a table and I'll bring you your coffee and a menu?'

'Thanks,' he said.

Looking around, he had plenty of choice of table, but he purposely took a window seat in the adjacent room near the fire, his back to both the bar and Melanie. He didn't trust his eyes in either respect, so instead stared out of a latticed window at a circle of car park illuminated by a single outside light.

A minute later Melanie reappeared, offering him a menu and reeling off a list of specials she had clearly memorised. Slim ordered a simple ham ploughman's with another coffee. As she took his order, Melanie said, 'So, did you find what you were looking for?'

'It's still ongoing,' Slim said. 'I had no other pressing engagements so decided to stay around a while.'

'You're up at the B&B?'

'Ah, yes.'

Melanie gave him a smile that could melt glaciers and inundate coastal communities. 'I thought I recognised your car. I do hope you'll stop by again before you leave.'

'Oh?'

She gave him a happy, almost pantomime sigh. 'There's not a lot going on around here. We don't get the tourists like the coastal towns do. Especially not at this time of year. And the walkers never have much to talk about.'

'I gather … you're not from around here?'

'London,' she said in an awkward cockney accent, which convinced Slim she was from one of the more affluent suburbs. 'I met Aaron at a tractor show, believe it or not.'

'You don't look like the kind of person to go to a tractor show. And I mean no offense.'

Melanie gave a dramatic pout. 'You have no idea. You know those scantily clad girls you get at motor racing events? Well, believe it or not, there's an agricultural equivalent. Except we wear overalls.'

'You were a … model?'

'Budding actress, actually. I had a few bit parts in sitcoms circa 2010. Blink and you'd miss it. The pay was crap, and I was working in a pub to pay the rent. Then I met Aaron and, well, you know what they say.'

'The rest is history.'

'That'll do. I miss the lights sometimes, but not the astronomical prices.'

'I can imagine.'

'So did you ever talk to William?'

'Not yet.'

Melanie smiled. 'It's not easy, bless him. Some days he's there, other days he's not.'

'I'd very much like the chance if I got it—'

The door opened with a creak of hinges and a sudden flurry of wind bustled inside. Melanie straightened. 'I'll get your food and your coffee.'

Slim looked out of the window as she went back to the bar. A moment later he heard her say, 'Hi, Brian, what can I get you?'

Slim couldn't resist turning around, and as he did so, he found Brian Tate, perched on a bar stool, already staring at him. Before Slim could move, Brian was on his feet.

'You're still here, are you?' he said. The amicability had gone from his tone as he took a couple of steps forwards. He looked burly, threatening. Slim had no choice but to stand or put himself at a disadvantage, and found himself squaring up to the old hunt master. Brian had the height, but Slim had the years. And while he had wasted himself for decades, he felt no fear from an old man. Getting into a bar fight, however, hadn't been on the schedule.

'I heard you came round my place asking questions,' Brian said. 'I gave you my time. Respect my privacy.'

'I just had a couple more. I had hoped to speak to your daughter.'

'You leave her alone.'

Brian had balled a fist and Slim feared the old man might unleash a wild haymaker. He inched towards the door; he had nothing to gain from this.

'I meant no offense. I just wondered what your daughter remembered of the night Elissa Lowescroft died. That's all. I'm sorry if my questions caused any distress.'

'Take your questions and sod off,' Brian said. 'She hasn't got nothing to say about all of that. Wasn't even there that day.'

'She wasn't?'

'Off sick. Had a cold. There. That enough for your book or whatever you're writing? You journalist types are all the same.'

'I think I'd better go,' Slim said, glancing at Melanie, who was hovering nearby, looking nervous. Brian's face was bright red, both fists balled now. The young couple had left but the other two customers were watching with interest.

Brian just glared at him. Slim backed through the door, then quickly walked away into the night, glancing back when he was a little way up the road to see if Brian had followed him, but through the pub window he could see the old man settling at the bar.

Slim sighed. It looked like he would need to drive to a local supermarket after all. He hoped he could find one that was open. He wondered too whether it was too late to give Victoria another call.

20

DARTMOOR WAS wild and wet the next morning as Slim climbed the hill to the dramatically positioned St. Michael's church. He found it more impressive for its three hundred-and-sixty-degree panoramic views than for its interior, which was cramped and unadorned.

Politely greeting a couple of other visitors on their way out, he went inside and made his way to the back, where he dropped a couple of pounds into a collection box and then flicked through the large visitor's book. From the scarcity of entries it was clear that the church was off the beaten tourist trail, and this book alone dated back to 2009. He wondered how he might view older books, but on a noticeboard inside the door he found the name and contact details for the current reverend.

From the steep hillside outside, he could see the V of the valley in which Elissa had died. As the crow flew it was half a mile from here, over relatively flat moorland with no field boundaries or obstructions bar a couple of small rocky protrusions. A fifteen-minute walk in decent weather, a ten-minute panicked run.

He was clutching at proverbial straws to think that she might have come here to the church in search of refuge during the six-hour period after her disappearance but before her death. After all, finding shelter, why would she have again left? In addition, from the church it was a short, simple walk down to the nearby road where there was a car park and even a toilet block. While the toilet might not have existed in 1982, the road certainly would have, and again, having found civilisation, Elissa would not have abandoned it again for no good reason.

Slim made a circuit of the church, observing the moor from all directions. On most sides the slope was gentle enough to be walked, but on one corner there was a steep drop off, with dangerous rocks below. Again, he reminded himself that Elissa's cause of death was asphyxiation, the only impact wound a light one from maybe striking her head as she fell down, not the kind of impact wound to suggest a greater fall.

He shook his head, frustrated. He had nothing except airy speculation. It looked like the official report might be correct after all, that she had wandered around on the moor for a while, before tripping, hitting her head, and suffocating in the waterlogged grass.

He squatted down, his back aching, and stretched out his legs on a patch of flat rock partially covered with grass.

No. There were too many open doors to give up now, even though his forehead was battered and bloody from knocking them all down. At the very least he needed to find some solid reason for the missing period between Elissa's disappearance and her death.

It wasn't impossible that she had wandered, lost and frightened, out across the moor while a thick fog rolled in and night fell. But to be found no more than two hundred yards from where she had last been seen … that made no sense.

What did make sense was that someone had killed her, then laid her body where it seemed most likely she could have naturally died.

But who? And how?

And most importantly, why?

21

'I DON'T SMOKE,' Morton Gale said, glaring at Slim across the table in the visitation room while a warden stood nearby.

'Nor do I,' Slim said, 'but I understand currency in prison. At least that was how it was the last time I was inside.'

Morton, a rough, stubbly-faced man with hard, grey eyes and a shaved head, lifted an eyebrow.

'You're an ex-con, are you? What did you do time for?'

Slim took a deep breath. 'Manslaughter by way of self-defense,' he said. 'That and a couple of other things. Intent to cause GBH. Drunk and disorderly. Affray.' He lowered his eyes. Saying the words out loud always hurt. 'Breaking and entering.'

Morton gave a dry chuckle. 'It looks like we're sitting on the wrong sides of the table,' he said.

Slim smiled. 'I don't remember anyone visiting me,' he said.

Morton cocked his head. 'This is a special occasion,' he said with a note of regret. 'The damn family deny my existence.' He leaned forwards and smiled. The glint of a silver filling made him into a caricature, but behind the frown and the hard jawline, Slim saw vulnerability in the way his eyes wavered, unable to stay still. Morton was doing a good impression of appearing not nervous, but not good enough.

'So,' Morton said. 'Who are you and what is it you want?'

'My name is John Hardy, but most people call me Slim.'

'We're on nickname terms, are we?'

'We're on whatever terms you want to be. I'm a private investigator. It's a long story how I came to be here, but the short end of it is that I'm investigating the death of Elissa Lowescroft. Friday, October 22nd, 1982. You both went on a school trip to Brent Tor, on the edge of Dartmoor. All I want to know is what you remember of that day.'

Morton stared at him for a long time. Slim began to think he was going to get up and leave, when Morton suddenly said, 'Elissa, is it? I expected something a little more recent. Elissa … you might not want to go digging there.'

'Why not?'

Morton's eyelids fluttered as he looked away into space.

'Elissa and me were mates.'

'Mates? Not friends?'

'Yeah, she was a total tomboy. Not in school—she wouldn't look at me in school—but outside. She used to come over to the cottage, get me away from Dad. We'd go out on the moors, go hunting for stuff. Rabbits, bird's nests, those little boxes they have hidden up there. Mostly just messing around. She was one for the hills, was Elissa. Probably would have lived in a cave if she could have.' He shrugged. 'We were just hanging around, though. Having a laugh.'

'I'm sorry if my questions are causing you to relive uncomfortable memories.'

Morton scoffed. 'My whole life is an uncomfortable memory. This is just one of many.'

'I've heard suggestions that her death might not have been as accidental as is claimed.'

'You and the rest of the outside world,' Morton said. 'But what can anyone prove after forty odd years?'

'Just give me something to go on, Morton,' Slim said. 'Anything. What do you remember from that day?'

Morton pushed his fists into his face then scratched at an ear. New scabs lined Morton's knuckles and for the first time Slim noticed the faded bruises around Morton's eyes.

'I was happy as a pig in shit,' Morton said. 'Hated school, especially that old witch Leddon. But it was better than being at home with Dad, you know what I mean?'

'He was abusive?'

'And the rest. Wasn't working much in those days, only when Uncle Jake would give him something to do on the farm to give him some pub money. Mum was supporting us, cleaning holiday cottages, the only job she could really do where no one would notice the bruises. She'd stay out as long as she could, keep out of his way, leave me to him. School was better than nothing, but a walk out on the hills on the clock was the best thing ever.'

'So you were in good spirits that day?'

'Yeah, hell yeah.'

'What about Elissa?'

'Didn't really think anything of it at the time, but after … after she disappeared, I thought she had seemed kind of brooding that day, you know what I mean? Like she had something important on her mind.'

'Like she had planned to run off all along?'

'I dunno about that,' Morton said. 'She wasn't stupid. Knew the dangers of the moor better than anyone.'

'What was your opinion of Philip Reece?'

Morton's sour pout followed by a scoff told Slim everything he needed to know. 'That clown? He didn't want anything to do with me. He always had his eyes on the girls.'

Slim leaned back in his chair. So often his investigations began with rumours he then had to evaluate. He sensed vitriol in Morton's voice and chose his words carefully, hoping to draw a little more.

'I've spoken to other people who knew him. They had nothing bad to say about him.'

'Only the girls would say that. He was all over them.'

'Are you saying he had … unlawful intentions towards them?'

'Say it how it is, won't you? He was a perv. Might not have done anything yet, but it was only a matter of time. Of course he went after Elissa when they realised she was lost. Probably spotted his chance.'

'And what was your opinion of what happened to him?'

'Covering it up. A couple of years in a nuthouse is better than life, isn't it?'

'What about how he died? You know it was a suicide?'

'Probably a set up. Someone got to him, didn't they?'

22

Slim had hoped for more information out of Morton, but his visitation time abruptly ended and he left the prison with more questions than answers. Philip Reece, whom he had previously written off as a possible suspect in any wrongdoing, now loomed large once more. Slim found himself wandering the streets of Plymouth, trying to make sense of everything, wishing the scattered pieces would just fall into place.

It was almost in desperation that he called Don.

'I'll see what I can find out,' Don said. 'I did look into Philip Reece, but found no prior convictions, nothing to suggest he might have had anything but good intentions when he went off to look for the girl.'

Slim had been putting off listening to the tapes of Reece's police interviews, even though Don had found the recordings that Simon Clifford had mentioned. Slim had already downloaded the files, so drove up on to the moor, found a desolate parking area, and opened his laptop.

He lasted no more than five minutes before having to switch off the first recording. Not so much for the content, but for the sheer frustration of trying to pick meaning out of what for the most part was white noise. Reece's screaming drowned out the police officer's questions with incomprehensible, machine gun howling and chattering, talking over himself, seemingly trying to give three accounts at once, none of which made sense. It was the sound of a madman; Slim had seen some good acts over the years, but if this was one, it was worthy of a prize.

He took a sip of coffee, a deep breath, then skipped the recording forward a few minutes. The voices had gone quiet. Someone was sobbing.

'What did you see, Philip?'

'I'm sorry. Tell her I'm sorry.'

'Was it someone you knew? Can you describe her?'

The sobbing continued. Slim really wanted a beer or a glass of wine, anything to take the edge off. He skipped forward a little more, then back a little to catch the end of a sentence.

'It's not fair, I didn't deserve this!'

Slim had had enough for now. He closed the laptop and drove back across the moor. He couldn't resist taking a detour, though, so took the road heading back through Postbridge.

It was getting dark. He drove through the little village, then pulled into a small parking area behind a stand of trees. He got out of the car and walked back down the road until Brian Tate's house came into view.

Slim pulled a small pair of binoculars out of his pocket and lifted them to his eyes.

Through a downstairs window he caught a glimpse of two people preparing dinner. Ginny was moving quickly back and forth, laying plates and cutlery. Brian was doing less, looking for all the world like a bothersome husband trying not to get in the way. Slim almost smiled as Ginny handed him a folded newspaper and pointed to a chair. Just as he moved to do so, however, Brian looked up at the window.

Slim froze, worried something might have glinted off the binoculars' lenses, possibly revealing him. In the dark and over the distance Brian had no chance of identifying him, so he stayed stock-still, watching as Brian came around the table to the window.

As Brian reached for the curtains on either side, he leaned close to the glass, neutralising the reflection in order to see outside. Instead of looking towards Slim, however, he looked down the hill towards the road, then up into the stand of woodland behind his house. He held each gaze for several seconds, his head tilted enough to give his intentions away.

Then, as Brian pulled the curtains closed, Slim lowered the binoculars. There was something in Brian's mannerisms that made Slim suspicious. Despite his brusque exterior, he was a nervous man, carrying, perhaps, a load of years-old guilt. Slim knew that somehow, he had to get inside the man's head.

He was about to head back to his car when a distant thud made him look up.

Brian had come out of his house and now stood on the front step. He stood for a few seconds, then walked quickly down the path in front of his house to a small front gate that opened onto the gravel driveway that led down to the main road.

Slim started to panic. If Brian took a walk, he only had to go a few hundred yards to discover Slim's parked car. It was dark, but the moon was out, giving spectral, silvery views out across the moor. Slim started to backtrack, but Brian abruptly turned in his direction, peering into the dark.

Slim froze again. Had a lifetime of running hunts given Brian some kind of extra level of perception? Or did he just know the moor well enough to recognise when something was amiss?

It felt like a face off. Maybe Brian had noticed a change in the outline of the trees he had seen so many times, the hint of a person standing there, afraid to move. Or perhaps he had just gone out for some air.

Brian opened the gate and stepped out on to the gravel path. He took a few steps in the direction of the main road, then stopped again.

A trickle of cold sweat ran down Slim's back. Not many cars must pass this way so late in the evening. Brian might be tuned to engine sounds and had heard someone stop. Slim had to get back to his car, but Brian was looking straight towards him. Any movement at all would give his position away.

And then the front door opened, a pathway of light stretching out into the garden.

'Dad? Dinner's ready,' Ginny called.

Brian paused a moment longer, then abruptly turned and walked back through the gate.

'Coming,' he called.

But just as he reached out to pull the gate closed, he paused once again. This time he looked directly towards where Slim stood, and Slim felt Brian's eyes boring into him.

As Brian headed back to the house, Slim let out a slow breath.

He had thought he was the hunter, but for a moment he had felt much more like a poor, doomed fox.

23

ALAN COAKER, an old Armed Forces colleague who now ran a security firm in London was his usual gruff self.

'I don't have any hope of getting paid for this, but any chance of at least a Christmas card this year?' he said, after Slim had explained what he required.

'You're on the list,' Slim said.

'With hundreds of others you owe, no doubt.' Then with a resigned sigh, Alan added, 'Give me a day or two.'

Slim gave Alan the address of a local post office, thanked him and then hung up.

Next, he tried to call Victoria Aldridge, but for the third time in the last couple of days his call went through to voicemail. Having left messages on the previous two occasions, this time he declined, afraid that the affability she had displayed during their first call might have been just a front.

It was getting too late to make any more calls, but Slim was too wired to sleep. He brewed some coffee and thought about walking down to the local pub again, although he knew he would lack the nerve to go inside.

Instead, he sat on the bed and began to leaf through the old workbooks of Elissa's that Brenda had lent him.

Almost immediately he knew there was nothing useful to be found here. They were maths books, page after page of scrawled sums, a few doodles, but otherwise little of any interest. Had Elissa's mother saved some English exercise books or diaries, he might have been able to get some insight into Elissa's character, but the lines of numbers and symbols told him nothing.

However, he remembered something another old friend had told him, about how it wasn't just the words alone that were an insight into someone's personality, but the way they were made. He ran a finger over a page of pencil markings more than forty years old, feeling the bumps and creases of the paper. Some were scored so hard they were almost like braille. Slim turned a couple of pages, but to his untrained eye they were just what they appeared, lines of mathematics equations written by a bored little girl.

He started to push the book away, then paused, frowning. He squinted at the bottom edge of the book.

A series of lines and curves ran along the bottom of the page, written in pencil. Seen on their own, they could have been doodles, but they all intersected with the bottom edge of the paper.

Slim turned the page and found more. He turned back, and found others, on nearly every page.

He turned to the front of the book. A scrawled line of black marker identified it as July 1982.

Slim wasn't much of a diarist, rarely writing so much as a shopping list. Even to him, though, it was clear that the marks were the top half of a line of words, and that they had been written in a peculiar style, with the bottom half somewhere else. It occurred to Slim that such a thing might have been done to achieve a level of secrecy.

Could he be looking at the forty-year-old secret diary of Elissa Lowescroft? And if he was, where was the other half?

He pulled out the other exercise books that Brenda had lent him and found other lines of marks. Interestingly, they were only found in the maths books. A couple of other exercise books had none.

Slim put the books aside and poured a coffee from the freshly made filter.

Several options presented themselves.

The lines of possible secret text had been written half along the bottom of the books and half along the tabletop. Maybe she had been writing insults to her teacher, a way of relieving her frustration, but something that could have been easily hidden. Had that been the case, though, there would surely have been deeper depressions in the paper from where the pencil had dropped the short distance to a lower surface, with the upwards strokes of some half-letters having similar indentations.

The answer was that Elissa had written across two books of a similar height, the true meaning of her words only understandable when the books were placed together.

And that only maths books had been used meant that she had done it only in a particular class.

In secondary school, where there were subject teachers, it could have meant the teacher was unobservant, the lesson easy, or that she had sat in a far corner of the room. In primary school, however, it had to be for a specific reason related to that subject, as the teacher was likely the same across all classes.

Slim rubbed his temples, trying to cajole his tired brain

into conjuring variables. Why maths class? And why keep the words secret?

He wandered over to the desk, where he had left some papers strewn across the work surface. He picked up the printout of the old class photo Don had found.

The answer was obvious.

The messages had been written across two exercise books, a way of sharing information silently, and they were not secret only to Elissa, but to another classmate, whoever had sat next to her in maths class.

24

'MOST OF IT'S THE SAME,' Simon Clifford said, 'but there are a couple of moments of clarity if you're willing to wade through it.' He reached into a bag and pulled out a thick folder. Offering Slim a grin, he said, 'But in case you aren't, I've printed you a transcript. It's highlighted and time-stamped in case you'd like to check out the more interesting parts for yourself.'

As Clifford pushed the folder across the table, Slim nodded. 'Thanks. I really appreciate it. I'll keep you in coffees until I'm finished with this.'

'I hope you find something. There are questions yet to answer, that's for sure.'

As Slim opened the file, Clifford leaned forwards.

'The best description of what Reece claimed to see is on page twelve.'

Slim flipped the pages over. A passage was highlighted halfway down.

Reece: A figure. Yes, I said that before. Are you listening?

PC Redfern: Can you describe her?

Reece: (*incoherent*) … eyes … she's watching me, oh god.

PC Davies: What about her eyes?

Reece: (*sobbing*) Yellow. So yellow. I'm sorry. I'm so sorry.

PC Davies: So the girl you saw had yellow eyes?

Reece: I should have been there. I'm so sorry.

Slim ran a finger down the page. Reece's answers became incomprehensible. He flicked forwards a few pages to another highlighted passage.

PC Redfern: Mr. Reece, can you confirm that when you went into the fog you didn't see Elissa Lowescroft?

Reece: A girl.

PC Redfern: But the girl wasn't Elissa?

Reece: Elissa?

PC Redfern: Did you see Elissa Lowescroft on Dartmoor after she went missing from the group?

Reece: Yellow eyes. Oh god I'm sorry.

PC Redfern: How close was this girl to you, Mr. Reece?

Reece: Come back. I'm sorry. Please don't leave me.

Slim looked up. 'It's like the babbling of a madman,' he said.

'If his testimony is true,' Clifford said, 'it's likely he had some kind of psychotic breakdown up on the moor, likely caused by some kind of phobia or past trauma. Certainly, what happened to him afterwards would suggest so. There's really very little to work with. I can tell you that now, but you're very welcome to pick through the interviews yourself. I'll gladly answer any questions you have, and if you find something I've missed, I'd love to hear it.'

Slim rubbed his chin. 'Through everything, the assumption is that he saw something up on the moor? A child?'

'If you pick it apart, you can come to that conclusion, yes. A child in a hat with yellow eyes but no nose or mouth. An apparition, maybe.'

Slim looked down. His finger traced a score mark in the tabletop. 'The ghosts that haunt most men come from inside,' he said. 'I've seen things … and I have my own ghosts. But they can be explained. Every last one of them.'

'You don't believe any of the stories about ghosts out on Dartmoor, then?' Clifford said with a smirk. 'You're not into ladies in wedding dresses floating down foggy stone paths?'

'The mind has a lot of tricks,' Slim said. 'It's certainly played its share on me. But disassociated beings … no. A ghost is a personal thing that comes from inside a person … and if it's not, it's something else.'

'How do you mean?'

'This case is closed,' Slim said. 'Elissa's death was ruled accidental. Philip Reece died in an institution, and George Stockwood had his career ruined. We could say there were three victims. Let's assume for a minute that everything Philip Reece claimed he saw was real, that he did in fact see a little girl out on the moor, in a hat and with yellow eyes but no nose or mouth. Who could that have been, and what might she have been doing out there that day?'

25

IN SEARCH OF MORE INFORMATION, Slim walked over to the public library and hunted out an old coffee table book showing views of Dartmoor from the air. Finding a picture that suited his needs, he painstakingly made colour photocopies of the oversized book, then taped them back together. Rolling the bundle into a tube, he headed back to the B&B.

There, he laid it out on the floor, took a marker pen, and began circling points of interest, including the car park, St. Michael's church, the valley of the River Burn tributary, and the site of Elissa's memorial.

It soon became apparent that his budding theory wouldn't fit. He had wondered at the distance to Brent Tor from Postbridge, but it was thirty minutes by road, and while crossing the moor was more direct, there was no obvious path. And while he had hoped to identify the residents of every dwelling within a mile radius, that would mean checking upwards of fifty houses.

Something was apparent, though. While walking eastwards would take a person up onto the moor, a short walk in any other direction would have quickly brought a person to a road. That Elissa hadn't swiftly found the safety of some mark of civilisation suggested that in part her actions had been intentional, or at least dictated by an external factor.

A yellow-eyed girl in a hat with no nose or mouth by any chance?

That it had been Philip Reece who had followed the girl that day seemed significant, and Slim clung like a drowning man to the theory that Elissa had run off intentionally to draw Reece away, to prank him, perhaps, or even something more sinister.

Had Reece been doing something bad to Elissa? Morton seemed to suggest the possibility, even if Victoria's testimony denied it.

He looked down at the map. He had circled where Elissa's hidden knife had been found. From the place she had disappeared, it made an even-sided triangle with the place where her body was found. The distance—as the crow flew—was around five hundred yards.

Had she decided to cut across the moor to retrieve the knife, then meet Reece somewhere back on the path as he came to find her?

Her body had been found near the river. There were several stands of trees nearby, any of which could have concealed her, particularly factoring in the fog.

She had never made it back to the knife, however. Somehow, she had gotten lost, remaining alive for another six hours before she died, her body found in the spongy grass up the hill from the stream where her memorial now stood.

Slim wanted to screw up the map and throw it away. Nothing made sense. None of it.

More than forty years had passed. Slim felt certain

someone else had been on the moor that day, but how could he possibly discover who after so many years?

He needed to narrow the possibilities. He had called the reverend of St. Michael's church, who had promised to look for any old visitor books. Simon Clifford had given him transcripts taken in the immediate aftermath from interviews with George Stockwood and also James Greg, the coach driver, both of whom claimed there had been no other cars in the car park that day. While it was of course possible someone had parked along the road, ridden up by bike or been illegally camping out on the moor, Slim would go out of his mind wondering about those.

The only other realistic possibility was a local, capable of reaching the area—and then retreating unseen —on foot.

Slim stared at the map again. There were several houses close enough that someone could have walked up to the moor, but most of them were to the west, on the other side of the main road. The convenient way would have been back down the road behind the car park.

The only other nearby dwellings were to the north. There were a pair of old council houses Slim remembered driving past which had now been converted to holiday lets. And a couple of hundred yards past those was the entrance to the narrow lane which made an arc down through a flat valley for a mile or so before reaching Gale Farm, nestled in a valley over to the northeast.

Slim stared for a long time. Had Elissa been alarmed by whatever Philip Reece had also seen, fled north, come to the lane, and attempted to take refuge at Gale Farm?

The distance was not impossible, and while the road she might have followed was now a major trunk road, on Slim's old map it looked far narrower, less inviting for traffic.

Aaron Gale would have been a toddler at the time, the farm run by his grandfather William and father, Jake. On a working farm, however, it was likely most of the men would have been out at work somewhere.

Had Elissa encountered someone on the farm? Had something tragic happened, something that had caused someone to conceal her body, someone who knew enough about the situation to later place Elissa where the search parties would find her?

When Slim saw it, he nearly jumped to his feet.

Of course.

Someone with a history of violence, who might have been idling around the farm that day, and who had knowledge of the school trip and later of the location of Elissa's disappearance.

Only one person fitted all the possibilities.

Morton Gale's father.

26

'Sᴏʀʀʏ not to get back to you,' Victoria said on the video call screen. 'I don't know if our last conversation spooked me or something, but I just found it hard relieving those days over again. You know, I've not been back to Devon since.'

Slim smiled. 'It's understandable. I'm sorry to have caused you any distress.'

'It's not that. It's just … it was a strange period of my life. One I rarely think about now. Since I spoke to you the first time, things have started to become clearer.'

'Do you remember any of the names you'd forgotten?'

Victoria smiled. 'Not that clear. Just … certain things. I remember it being bitterly cold, even before the fog rolled in. I remember Mr. Stockwood saying to Ms. Leddon that they should have put gloves on the permission slip and her snapping back at him that it would warm up. I remember Morton had a pair that had a label still attached and someone—I forget who—said he'd probably pinched them.'

'I wanted to ask you if you remembered the name of

the girl who was absent that day. The girl you said was your friend.'

Slim had deliberately embellished what Victoria had told him before.

'I didn't say she was my friend,' Victoria said, taking the bait. 'She was nice to me, though.'

'Isn't that the same thing?'

'It depends. She was friendly. We didn't hang out in the playground or anything like that.'

'Why not?'

'Because she was Elissa's friend. When Elissa wasn't around though … I did feel we could have been friends. We sat next to each other in science, for example. We did experiments together, and it was cool. In the playground, though, she was in Elissa's group, and I certainly wasn't.'

'Sorry, you didn't tell me her name.'

'Oh. Jane … no, Ginny … Ginny Tate.'

Slim gave a slow nod. So, Brian had been telling the truth. Rather than removing Ginny from any of his suspicions, however, it gave rise to another, far darker possibility.

He glanced past the screen at the map he had left lying on the floor. The distance between Postbridge and Brent Tor was significant, not one that could be easily walked, especially by a child. And there were no direct roads, only a long, circuitous route.

However, there was another way.

'I have one more question, Victoria, if that's all right. Then I'll let you get on with your day. Could Ginny ride?'

'A horse, you mean?'

'Yes.'

Victoria nodded. 'Of course. She was in Elissa's riding club. I don't think she was as good, but she certainly knew what she was doing.'

27

'I'LL GIVE YOU THAT, Slim. You're good. All these years, I never thought of it.'

'I'm not sure how I could prove it without a confession, but the circumstances would work,' Slim said. 'Elissa had planned to prank Philip Reece, perhaps scare him. She ran off and had him follow, only to meet Ginny, who had taken the day off school and then ridden across the moor from Postbridge, in some kind of disguise. She scared him, then rode back across the moor. Depending on how she planned it, her father Brian might not have even known.'

'I admit it's a decent theory. However, that's all it is unless Ginny comes clean. And it still doesn't explain what happened to Elissa.'

'No, it doesn't. I wondered about some kind of accident, maybe involving the horse, but the timeline doesn't agree, nor do the reports of her supposed injuries. However, I have another theory.'

'Go on.'

'What if Ginny's involvement was totally random? What if she had ridden out to Brent Tor that day just for fun, or maybe just to have a look at her class from a distance. The fog might not have rolled in until she was halfway there. Perhaps in a panic herself, she had surprised both Philip Reece and Elissa. We know what happened to Reece, but what if Elissa had also fled, heading north, finding herself on the lane that leads up to Gale Farm?'

Simon nodded. 'I think I see where you're leading with this. She ran into Nathan Gale, right?'

'It's possible. He was out of work, and his family was living on the property at the time. It's possible something happened, then later he took Elissa's body back to the moor.'

'He would have known about the trip through Morton, and might have heard that Elissa had gone missing. Slim, you could be on to something.'

'How I would prove this, I don't know. I would really like to speak to Morton's mother, if she's still alive, and if I can get a confession out of Ginny Tate, I might have something circumstantial to work with. Even if I can't force the case to be reopened, it might at least offer some closure to Elissa's mother.'

'Keep me posted, Slim. And if there's anything I can do to help, let me know. I'll try to find out what happened to Morton's mother, but the best option would probably be to ask Morton yourself.'

Slim offered a grim smile. 'I'm not sure how easy that'll be, nor if he even knows. I got the impression she hasn't kept in touch.'

After they parted ways, he headed back to his B&B. It was just after three o'clock, and as he drove past the pub he saw Melanie Gale come outside, collect some glasses from a wooden bench, then head back inside. He hesitated only a moment before pulling into the car park.

The pub was empty besides a family just paying up as

he headed inside. Somehow the sights and smells of the place were easier to deal with during the day, but as he waited for Melanie, he repeated a mantra over and over in his mind that he was driving, he couldn't drink. Even though it was only a five-minute walk to his B&B, he couldn't, wouldn't drink.

As soon as she was finished with the family Melanie came over, a worried look on her face.

'Slim,' she said. 'I wondered if you'd stop in again. I'm so sorry about the other night. I don't know what got into Brian. He's usually so friendly.'

'I think we got off on the wrong foot,' Slim said.

'Can I get you a drink?'

'Ah … just … coffee. Thank you.' He gripped the edge of the bar to hide the tremble in his hands. As she turned to a coffee machine behind the bar, he sighed and let go.

'Just a sec,' Melanie said, not looking back. 'I'll just put on a new filter.'

'Just microwave what you've got left,' Slim said. 'That's how I like it. Brewed yesterday if possible.'

'If you're sure.'

'I am.'

He settled down at the bar, more comfortable once Melanie had placed the drink in front of him as it eased the craving for another.

'Brian didn't scare you away, then?' Melanie asked, leaning back against the counter behind the bar and folding her arms. She wore a smile as though it were a joke, but Slim had come close to wearing one of Brian's haymakers and found it difficult to smile back.

'Not the first time I've upset the locals,' he said. 'I doubt it'll be the last.'

'Surely a bit of ghost hunting can't be that intrusive?'

Slim grimaced. 'It depends whose ghost you're hunting.'

'I'm not from round here, but I've always gathered that Elissa Lowescroft was a particularly bitter one.'

'In what way?'

'A lot of blame going around. And you know how these embedded local families can be. They've all got a skeleton in the closet somewhere.'

'Was Nathan Gale the skeleton in the Gale family's closet?' Slim asked, trying to keep his tone light, almost casual. 'I've heard he was quick with his fists and slow with his work.'

He was intentionally embellishing the rumours that he had heard, giving Melanie a chance to correct him. She just shrugged.

'You might have noticed Aaron's not much of a conversationalist,' she said. Then, tilting her head and giving him a photogenic smile, she added, 'But I'm a lot better with it. Promise to stop by and keep me company on Tuesday or Wednesday afternoon, and I'll try to squeeze something out of him.'

Life had hardened Slim, but not so much that he couldn't melt at least a little in the presence of a beautiful woman. She was disarming, something he knew was dangerous, but he was an insect, flying intentionally into the trap.

'Sure,' he said.

'So, while you're here, you remember that programme they did about the corrupt banker? How on earth did you know it was the ex-wife's sister?'

28

Audrey Johnson couldn't keep the surprise off her face.

'Mr. Hardy? I didn't expect to see you again.'

'May I come in?'

'Sure. Andy's up in his room. Would you like to talk to him?'

'Maybe, in a while.'

Over a coffee he explained that while he couldn't make any promises, nor would he accept any more of Audrey's money, he hadn't yet closed down his investigation.

'You might hear from me again, or you might not,' Slim said, wishing the coffee was a little stronger after another night of fitful sleep. 'I won't bother you unless I find anything. And at the moment, I don't have any concrete leads.'

'Thank you anyway for your efforts.'

Slim nodded, wondering how much she might thank him if he dug too deep.

'I do have a request,' he said.

'Sure. Anything.'

'These bears Andy makes for the memorial. May I borrow one?'

Audrey looked briefly taken aback. 'Ah, sure.'

'I can't promise that I'll be able to return it.'

'Well, he churns them out so I don't think he'll mind.'

'Thanks.'

They made small talk for a while until the coffee was done, mostly Audrey asking questions and Slim deflecting them with vague answers. It felt like a delaying action, but finally Slim stood up and said, 'Can we see Andy now?'

Audrey nodded, then led him upstairs without looking back. On the landing, Audrey knocked on a closed door.

'May I come in?'

There came a muffled answer Slim couldn't hear. Audrey turned to him with a pained look and said, 'He's on the phone.'

The disconnected phone was part of the charade of Andy's life. Slim just nodded. A moment later there came a louder call from inside.

'Enter.'

Slim followed Audrey into the room. He had been in here briefly earlier in his investigation, but not while Andy had been present. Even then it had both impressed and shocked, but with Andy here it felt even more impressive yet at the same time tragic.

What had once been a medium-sized bedroom had been transformed into a cluttered office and workspace.

There was a bed hidden behind a doctor's screen, and Slim caught a glimpse of a childlike bedside table loaded with children's toys and picture books. In front of the screen, however, was structured, organised chaos. A large desk was pushed against the opposite wall to the bed, a bookshelf covering half of a window that looked out onto the street was loaded with books on business and self-development. On the desk were three computers, all running the same rotating nature-themed series of screensaver pictures. To see all three change in perfect precision was so disconcerting that Slim had to look away.

A landline hung from the wall that was covered in annotated calendars, work schedules, and planners. At first it seemed relevant to whatever Andy thought he was doing, but as Slim looked closer, among other things he recognised a timetable for Exeter St. David's Station, a bus route chart for Plymouth city centre, and also a daily feeding schedule for the animals at Paignton Zoo.

Everything had been arranged in a kind of artistic symmetry. None of the poster edges touched each other. The gaps of wall between them were regular distances apart. Even the pins in the corners were uniform, all the same design, all embedded at what Slim felt sure was an exact measurement from the corners.

Even the books on the shelves showed signs of obsessive-compulsive disorder. Lined up in pairs of the same height, they made little steps up from the lowest pair to the highest. Even the computers were arranged at regular angles, the phone on the wall perfectly straight.

The disorder came with Andy. He held a pad of tatty paper in one hand, the corners curled as though he had massaged them with his fingers. He held a pencil in the other hand and was making marks on the paper. Slim leaned closer and recognised line after line of neat crosses lined up so regularly it could have been a printout from a computer. Something in his heart broke.

'Mr. Jenkins from Derbyshire Street called to make a second order,' Andy said with total honesty, tapping his pencil against the paper as he looked up at Audrey. 'I'm wondering if we have the inventory to fulfill it.'

Audrey gave her adult son a pat on the arm. 'I'm sure

we do,' she said. 'You put in the order to the supplier, didn't you?'

'Of course.'

'Then there's no need to worry.'

'I know.'

'Ah … Andy, this is Mr. Slim, do you remember him?'

Andy looked at Slim, but his gaze seemed to pass right through Slim with a blank expression and gummy eyes. He nudged spectacles without lenses a little further up his nose.

'Are you a returning customer?' Andy said.

Slim quickly got himself into character and nodded. 'Yes,' he said. 'Yes, I am. I was happy with my … previous order, so I wanted to order again.'

Andy's smile was like the glossy, airbrushed expression of a billboard advert.

'That's great news. Have you checked out our full range of products?'

Slim glanced at a smaller desk behind Andy, one which more closely resembled a textiles workshop. Two baskets of assorted material pieces, wool, stuffing, and thread framed the half-finished body of a little blue teddy bear, a needle still sticking out of its chest like a sacrificial knife.

'I have,' Slim said. 'I'd like to order one of those little bears if I may.'

Andy's smile dropped. 'I'm afraid we're out of stock,' he said.

The look in Andy's eyes was unsettling. Slim wanted to look away but forced himself to hold Andy's gaze.

'Can you make one to order?'

Andy shook his head. 'Full production capacity has been reached,' he said.

'I'm not in any hurry.'

Andy shook his head. 'Impossible. You should try another manufacturer.'

Slim sensed further argument would get him nowhere, and was about to retreat, when Audrey lifted a hand.

'What about one of the returns?' she said, pulling open a drawer in Andy's desk before he could stop her. 'Surely he could have one of those?'

Andy's sudden wail was like the howling of a police siren. He kicked the drawer shut and began to spin on the chair, hands clamped over his ears. It took only a glance from Audrey to tell Slim he needed to leave the room, but as he stepped back on to the landing, leaving Audrey to deal with her son, he could only think about what he had briefly seen in the drawer before Andy's swinging foot had slammed it shut.

A pile of muddied, sodden teddy bears, each one with its formerly smiling mouth remodeled to be downturned into an image of misery and sadness.

29

Despite Slim's protestations, Audrey insisted that she knew how to deal with Andy's episodes and bundled him out of the house. She promised to call him later, so he headed back to his B&B to hole up for a while.

He tried to sit and go through some notes, but he couldn't stay still. He paced about the room until the elderly landlady came upstairs and politely told him his footfalls were annoying the guests in the room below.

Filled with restless energy, he went outside and walked up through the village in the direction of the moor.

Had he really seen what he had thought he had seen?

The bears Andy made were happy, smiling things, the angular stitches on their faces upturned in childlike grins. The ones in the drawer, however, had mouths that angled downwards, with the new smiles stitched over the old in a more assured, practiced pattern. The buttons that made up the eyes, too, had been given extra stitches along the bottom edge to depress them, make them appear downturned in misery.

Was it possible that Andy had done it himself? Perhaps

as part of his delusion? Or was someone taking the bears he had made, altering them, and leaving them for Andy to find?

It was another lead, but one that still had the potential to go nowhere. What if what was happening to Andy was nothing more than an elaborate prank?

Slim found himself walking farther out across the moor. It was a pleasant day, the sky clear, the sun bright, the October chill briefly banished. Slim walked up the nearest peak whose name he had forgotten. In the distance the English Channel glittered, while inland St. Michael's church rose out of the landscape like an ancient alien monolith.

Slim jumped as the phone in his pocket buzzed, pulling him out of his thoughts.

Kay Skelton, an old Armed Forces friend who now worked as a forensic linguist. Slim had sent him one of Elissa's old exercise books to see if he could make any sense of the markings on the bottom of the books.

'Kay. Any luck?'

'Hey, Slim. Do you know how much I appreciate it when you send me something that actually falls within my area of expertise for a change? I've got something for you.'

'What is it?'

'Well, I collated the marks on the bottom of that book, then ran them through a program to tell me what the rest of the text would have been.'

'You have programs that can do that?'

'Welcome to the digital age. Of course, I could figure out most of it, but one or two words were a little vague. You were right, it appears the messages were written across two books pressed together. In possession of both, the text would be easy to read, but split in half would make it look like idle doodling. From the content, my guess is that the intent was to hide secret messages from a teacher.'

'Do you know what they say?'

'Yes. They're pretty juvenile. But we're talking about children, aren't we?'

'Nine-year-olds.'

Kay chuckled. 'All right. Sounds about it. The first one reads "Can you smell that? I think Danny just guffed."'

Slim couldn't help but smile. 'That's a word I've not heard in thirty years.'

'Right. There are plenty more. "Lizzie's got a poo stain on her dress."' Kay sighed. 'The next one I think is Martin?'

'Could be Morton.'

'Ah, right. I wondered about that "I". The tone is a little different for this one. It says "Morton's only got marg sandwiches again. Halves on a Penguin?"'

'I think she means those chocolate bars,' Slim said. 'And "marg" would be margarine.'

'You know of this person Morton?'

'Yes, her classmate. He grew up … underprivileged.'

'I got that impression. There are other coded messages too. I've made you a list.'

'Thanks. Can you send it to my email?'

Kay chuckled. 'Welcome to the modern world. How are you adjusting?'

'Slowly.'

'Well, keep trying.'

'I will.'

By the time he got back to the B&B, Kay had sent the email. The list was longer than Slim had expected but lacked any real actionable substance. In short, it was a list of childish jokes and jibes aimed at other pupils and the class teacher Margaret Leddon, no doubt written to amuse an idle mind during an unpopular subject. Elissa came across for the most part as unsympathetic, a little spiteful, a little spoiled. Slim didn't blame her; at times he had been the scourge of his own school playground, preferring to be the first to throw the punches, the last to get hit. While modern culture might have cleared many of the playground minefields it had once been necessary for every school pupil to negotiate, in 1982 it would have been the same traumatic rite of passage he had himself experienced. Elissa had used her family background and achievements to establish her position, just as he had used his fists to establish his.

The only time the carefully cultivated guard was lowered, however, was when she talked about Morton. Clearly the disadvantaged boy had been held in high esteem. He suffered none of the jokes and jibes that the other kids got, and when mentioned it was with a sense of pity. "Morton forgot his coat. I'll lend him mine if I can borrow your spare." "Did you see the bruise on Morton's shoulder this morning? He said he tripped. Yeah, right."

So, Elissa was a typical nine-year-old, it seemed, playful at times, occasionally nasty, but with a soft centre when it came to those close to her. Slim felt he had learned everything and nothing at the same time.

As he read over the messages, he tried to remember that these were just a snapshot of the relationship between the two girls, that they would have seen each other in breaks and before school. Each comment could have been a starter for a much longer playground conversation now long forgotten in the mists of time.

There were twenty-five comments. Slim read them all

over several times, searching for any significance, before giving a smile at his own seriousness. He was looking at the memory of two girls at play, nothing more.

But there was always something. Wasn't there?

Slim sighed. Brenda or Robina might have more old exercise books, but how could he ask for them without feeling embarrassed, without feeling like he was wasting their time?

And then he saw it, practically waving its hands at him, flashing lights and alarms blaring all over the place.

Two from the end:

I'm going to ride out there again tonight and take another look.

30

'MORTON, PLEASE.'

The other man shook his head. 'You leave her alone. She's got nothing to tell you.'

'How do you know? You were a child.'

'Don't patronise me. My old man might have been a savage, but he was no murderer.'

'Not everyone who kills means to do it,' Slim said. 'Believe me, I know.' He leaned forwards. 'And I think you know, too. The man you stabbed wasn't meant to die, was he, Morton? You just wanted to mess him up a bit.'

Morton stood up. 'We're done. Don't come here again.'

Slim stood up too, catching a reaction from the guard nearby. He had hoped not to have to play his trump card so soon, but Morton had left him no choice.

'I have a friend,' he said. 'I hear you've been denied parole twice. I can't promise, but I can try.'

Morton stopped. His back heaved. When he turned back, his eyes were red.

'Get me that hearing,' he said. 'Then we'll talk.'

Slim grimaced inwardly. He had hoped for the other way around. It wouldn't be an easy phone call to make.

'Sure,' he said. 'I'll be in touch.'

Morton flapped a hand at him, then Slim grimaced again as he watched his lead walk through a door at the end of the room.

Ben Holland, now highly ranked in the police, had been Slim's squad leader. "Friends" was an optimistic term, but as Slim had pulled himself out of the wreckage of his life and embarked on a career that continued to attract new plaudits, Ben had developed a grudging respect for the man he had once disciplined for being drunk on guard duty, and had been required to provide a character statement for when Slim's short-lived Armed Forces career came to an abrupt end. Slim had never seen the contents of that statement, but guessed it had contained reluctant praise, for he had received simply a dishonourable discharge rather than face criminal charges. And Ben, it seemed, had never forgiven him.

'John,' Ben said, his voice cool, unwelcoming. 'This isn't a courtesy call is it?'

'No.'

'It never is. What do you want this time?'

He went back to his B&B and his maps. As Elissa had disappeared during a school trip, Slim had paid little attention to where she had lived at the time. Her mother now lived Lamerton, but Slim remembered Robina saying the family had moved. He called her and arranged another meeting.

'We lived in that one there,' Robina said, looking at the map Slim had laid out and pointing at a detached house down a twisting lane just outside the village of Merrivale. She gave Slim a wistful smile. 'It was supposed to be our forever home. It was a bit tumbledown when we bought it, and we spent years fixing it up. My husband Gordon worked in Tavistock, so the commute was easy. After Elissa died, though, we fell out of love with it. I mean, we stayed there another ten years, but we only did what was necessary for the upkeep. After cancer took Gordon, and Brenda went off to university, I sold the place off and downsized.'

'She was into riding, wasn't she?' Slim said, stating what he already knew. 'Did you keep a horse in your garden there?'

It was a dumb question but intentionally so, and provoked the reaction Slim had hoped for. Robina laughed.

'Not at all. She used to go up to the Kirkwood Riding School in Willsworthy, near Gale Farm. It's gone now. Janine Kirkwood got too old to run it and sold it off. The old stables were all converted into holiday cottages.'

'Where would it have been?'

Robina pointed at a cluster of buildings down a narrow lane just south of Gale Farm.

'This was it.'

'Did Elissa go up there often?'

'Oh, yes. She spent more time up there than she did here, to tell the truth. In the holidays she was up there every day. Gordon used to drop her off on the way to work. Quite often she'd stay up there overnight too. I remember wondering who she thought her mother was, me or Janine, but she did love her horses.' She sighed. 'I often wish Brenda had been into them too. We never knew what to do with her in the holidays.'

'Was there ever any trouble up there? Did Janine ever have problems with Elissa?'

Robina shook her head. 'None at all. It made me terribly jealous at times. I felt like I was losing my daughter.'

31

'I CAN'T FIND ANYTHING,' Don said. 'My guess is that Morton's mother remarried or otherwise changed her name, perhaps to distance herself from her family. It's not impossible that if her son was involved with gangs she was put into some kind of witness protection program. Something like that is beyond even me, though. You're going to have to butter Morton up if you want to talk to his mother.'

Slim grimaced. 'I'm working on it. Any news on Philip Reece?'

'Some. I've found a cousin. Trying to get a bit more information. I need a few more days.'

'Sure. I appreciate it. And could you have a look into a Janine Kirkwood for me? She ran a riding school that Elissa attended. The school is long gone, and it's likely she's dead by now, but just in case. My contact didn't know what happened to her after the riding school closed.'

'Sure. Give me what details you have.'

Slim hung up and went back to his maps. He ran a finger over the paper, assessing the distances between each.

Elissa's body found here. The car park here. St. Michael's church, Gale Farm, Kirkwood Riding School, here, here, and here. And then, way out across the moor, Brian and Ginny Tate's place out at Postbridge.

He sighed. He had nothing at all. Not a thing he could prove, nothing other than some idle speculation.

He turned to the pile of material, buttons, thread and sewing equipment piled on the end of the bed. The half-finished teddy bear was of embarrassing quality, perhaps something a child in primary school would struggle to maintain much pride for. It was harder than it looked and even reaching Andy's quality had been tough for a man who had barely touched a needle since the first Gulf War. Still, it looked like what it was supposed to be, and it would do the trick.

It was time to break the case open.

He left his car in a small roadside car park a good mile from Postbridge and walked along the dark moorland road to where Brian Tate lived. The sky was clear, the moorland lit by moonlight. Slim saw only two cars, the headlights telegraphing them early enough that he was able to get off the road and out of sight long before they shrieked past.

He wore his thick coat and a woollen hat against the late October cold. He wore gloves too, hands stuffed into his pockets, the fingers of one hand encircling the little paper bag inside which he had placed the homemade blue teddy bear.

He had picked his date carefully. October 22nd, just a week before Halloween, was the 42nd anniversary of Elissa's death.

Andy had placed his toy earlier in the day, Audrey had said in a phone call, slipping out on the pretense of a business meeting and riding up to the moor on an electric bicycle she had recently acquired. Slim had already been to check, and had left some surveillance gear up there that Coaker had sent him.

Now, in his hand he carried more, not in the bear which was likely to be examined closely and probably swiftly discarded, but glued into a fold in the paper bag, which he expected to face far less scrutiny.

It was approaching midnight. The house was dark, barring an outside light casting a dim glow over the garden path and flowerbeds. This in itself disconcerted Slim, who had hoped to approach under complete darkness. Maybe it would be better to leave the package by a back door, or even hanging from the gate?

He was certain that Brian Tate and his daughter were hiding something. The bear would shock them into a reaction, he hoped, one that might reveal some part in the mystery.

He stood in the shadow by the road, pondering what to do. He was already having second thoughts, wondering if perhaps this wasn't too extreme an action, that he might be targeting innocent people. Had the drink still been fueling him, he would have executed his plan without question. Now, though, he begun to doubt himself.

And then a shadow appeared around the side of the house, a torchlight flickering.

Slim dropped to the ground. Peering through the metal bars of the gate, he recognised Brian Tate, carrying a box in one hand and a torch in the other, walk around to the front of the house, then start down the path.

Slim could do nothing other than shuffle away from the

gate and crouch down, pressing himself against the stone wall as Brian approached.

The gate creaked as Brian lifted the latch and stepped out onto the road. One twist of the torch and he would reveal Slim crouched there like a Peeping Tom, embarrassingly caught in the act. He already knew they would have some kind of confrontation; there would be no explaining away this situation as a chance encounter. But as Slim held his breath, Brian turned left, heading down the road to the river and the little road bridge that gave the village its name.

Slim gave him a chance to get a decent start, then waited for a billow of wind to run to the moorland across the road. There, he found the cover of some moorland rocks which would shield him from Brian's torch. There was no question of making a break for his car; whatever Brian was doing down at the bridge at midnight on the anniversary of the night Elissa died was not something he could miss.

Brian was a shadow farther down the road, the flicker of torchlight pooling in the road at his feet. Just short of the bridge he turned off the road and walked a short way back across the grass to an outcrop of granite poking out of the grass.

Slim crept closer. Brian's torchlight illuminated the box, then a moment later a flame flickered into life.

He was lighting a candle. Carefully, Brian placed the little round candle on top of the rock, in a small hollow safe from the wind.

It had to be for Elissa. But, as Slim watched, Brian lit another, then a third. At last there were five, nestled into the hollow in the rock.

Brian stood for a moment, then said something

inaudible under his breath. Then a moment later, he blew them out.

With the torch switched off, Brian was invisible in the dark. Slim held his breath, smelling the faint scent of burned candle wax.

Then, a voice, raised to be heard over the gusting wind, called, 'I know you're there. You can come out now.'

32

'I LOOKED YOU UP,' Brian said, standing a short distance away from Slim in the dark. 'I did my own research, I suppose. And those documentaries gave away far too much about you.'

'None of it was authorised,' Slim said. 'It's all for entertainment.'

'I'm a hunt master,' Brian said. 'Stalking and tracking is what I do. I could have called the police, but they did nothing the last time I needed them, so I had little hope of any help this time around. I know you're no threat to me, though. Thank the documentaries for that.'

'It's the night Elissa died,' Slim said.

'I know it is,' Brian said with a long sigh. 'It's also the night Jake crashed his car into these rocks.'

'Jake? You mean Jake Gale?'

'Yes. Who else?'

'I heard about his accident ... I didn't know he died the same night that Elissa went missing.'

Brian grunted. 'Your research missed that, didn't it? But you're right, in one respect, at least. He didn't die that night. He was in intensive care for a month before he passed away.'

Slim looked at the outcrop of rock. It was at a right-angle to the road, about thirty feet away, across a bumpy section of moor dotted with other rocks. Several of them could have slowed the car or deflected it, meaning Jake had to have been traveling at a high speed.

'These candles are for Jake?' Slim asked.

Brian let out a chuckle that was jarring in the night air.

'Good god, no,' he said. 'You think I'd light a candle for that animal?' He shook his head. 'These are for his victims.'

Slim's mind reeled. He had come here to break open Elissa's case, but it looked like he had managed to break through one layer of ice, only to find jagged shards underneath, ready to impale him. He had heard talk of Jake Gale's crash, both Lilian Taylor and Simon Clifford mentioning it in passing, but that it had occurred so close to Elissa's death … that was alarming. Was there a possibility that the two were connected?

'I need to know,' Slim said quietly.

'You're a coffee drinker, aren't you?' Brian said. 'I learned that about you too.'

'Are you?'

'Same. Is it too late for you?'

'It's never too late.'

'Come on then.'

They went up to the house. Brian let them in through a back door and into a cottage kitchen with slate flooring and bare stone walls. A few modern appliances looked out of place alongside a Rayburn built into one wall.

Brian pointed at a closed door. 'The girl's asleep upstairs. She won't hear us. Sleeps like a log, that one.'

'I don't want to disturb her.'

'You won't. Not unless you come around with any more questions. I'm talking to you now so that you'll leave my girl alone.'

'I can't promise that. It depends where my investigation leads.'

'You can and you will, or you walk back out into the dark and what I have to say stays unsaid.'

Slim sighed. 'All right.'

'The coffee's old. I'll make a new one.'

'Old is good. You have a microwave?'

'No. But I have a saucepan.'

Slim had never had coffee reheated in a saucepan before, but it tasted strong and bitter. 'Thanks,' he said, taking a sip as he sat across a dining table from Brian. 'Tell me about Jake Gale.'

'He ran a class for kids. Kind of like scouts for both boys and girls. He was into the girls, but the boys were a decent cover.'

Slim wrinkled his nose. 'Jesus Christ.'

'I don't know how far he got. He was a coward, you know? I don't know if he'd got to fiddling them or was still building up to it, but one night my Gin came home in tears saying she didn't want to go back. He'd been helping her put on a rucksack and let his hands wander. I didn't want to believe it, but my girl wasn't much of a talker. Still isn't. Must have taken a lot for something like that to come out. Now, her mother was long gone, so it was just me and her. I wasn't going to let something like that pass.'

'You confronted Jake?'

'That was the plan, yeah. I called up Jake's wife, she said he'd gone out on the moor. Gin was supposed to be at school but was feeling under the weather, so I left her in the house with the television on, then I went out there and waited for him. I was out there for hours, sitting on that rock, just waiting, going over what I might say or do.'

'You caused the crash?'

Brian chuckled. 'Good god, no. Postbridge and its legends did that. I just went out there to flag him down. We knew each other. If he hadn't have stopped when he saw me in the road, I'd have known he was hiding something. And if he did, I'd have had it out of him. Instead, he came along there way faster than you should be driving at that time of night. I don't know if he even saw me, but he went straight off the road and into those rocks.'

'You called the police?'

Brian lowered his eyes. 'When I saw the crash, at first I didn't want to. I wanted to go back home, go to bed, pretend I knew nothing of it. Because Gin had been off sick, I didn't know anything about Elissa's disappearance at that point, didn't hear about that until it was mentioned on Radio Devon in the morning, after they had found her. I figured sooner or later someone else would drive past, call it in, but I couldn't resist. I had to see what state he was in. I went over there, saw he was all beat up and unmoving. I thought he was dead. Honestly. And something in me … broke. I'd known him. We'd never been close friends, but we'd enjoyed a pint together from time to time. And I found myself doubting what my own daughter told me. I called the police, waited out there on the road for them to show up.'

'And this was the same night Elissa disappeared?'

'Yes. As I said, I didn't know that at the time, but it took the emergency services a long, long time to arrive, even for somewhere remote like out here. Not many to spare that night, and that was probably what did for him.'

'But they came in the end?'

'Eventually. About forty-five minutes after the crash, I'd say.'

'And Jake was alive?'

'Yes, but unconscious.'

'And he died later?'

'After a month or so. I don't know the exact date. They took him to Plymouth, had him in intensive care. His life support was switched off when they realised there was no more they could do.'

Brian sighed, rubbing tired eyes, but Slim, jolted awake by the coffee and revelations, leaned across the table.

'What else? There's more, Brian. I can see it on your face.'

Brian sighed. 'The lad was in the back. Aaron. I didn't even see him there, and he didn't cry, nothing. Broken glass had cut his face, but I think it had sent him into shock. I didn't even know until the police said. They pulled him out of that wreck alive, but by all accounts, he was never the same again.'

33

It was almost dawn when Slim left Brian Tate's house and headed back to his B&B. So wired from drinking coffee all night, he lay awake on his bed for a while before falling asleep just after sunrise. He woke again with a sore head around lunchtime, his stomach growling.

Brian, clearly unchained from confessing his part in Jake Gale's fatal car crash, had wanted to talk. Armed with this new knowledge, Slim called Simon and arranged a meeting with him at their regular café in Tavistock. Simon arrived just after three o'clock. Slim was already two coffees and a sandwich deep, his mind reeling with fresh information. On the surface, he could see no connection at all to Elissa's possible murder, but he couldn't ignore the possibility when two such dramatic events had happened on the same night.

Brian had elaborated about his claims somewhat, but on the condition that Slim withhold his name. Where he could be, Slim was a man of his word.

'I wanted to talk about Jake Gale's car accident,' Slim said. 'I understand it happened late on the same night

Elissa died. You never mentioned it. Could it have been possible that the two events were linked?'

Simon shook his head. 'Until you came up with your theory about Nathan Gale and Elissa, I'd never seen any possible connection at all. Of course, the coincidence was significant, but that's all. It was a car crash, in a pretty notorious place for them. One that left a sour note in many people's mouths, namely because so much of the local resources were allocated to searching for Elissa that had they not and authorities arrived sooner, Jake could possibly have been saved. Now we'll never know.'

'But in a sleepy little place like here, two such events like that on the same night? You can't blame me for wondering.'

Simon gave a grim smile. 'Some claimed that the Postbridge ghosts were riled up, that night,' he said.

'So the general opinion was that Jake might have been saved had emergency services arrived sooner?'

Simon shrugged. 'Who knows? I'm not an expert on it. I do know that he was supposedly driving too fast on a section of road that doesn't allow for it, and he suffered significant head injuries.'

'And the boy was in the car?'

'Aaron? Yes.'

'But he survived?'

'He was strapped into a child seat. It wasn't fitted properly on the inside strap and twisted in the impact, turning to face the rear of the car.'

Slim nodded thoughtfully. It could explain why Brian had failed to see the child.

'I can tell what you're thinking,' Simon said. 'You think there was some link between the two events. Believe me, there wasn't a journalist around here who didn't think it at the time. It was just too much of a coincidence.'

'But nothing came of it?'

'No. We considered every avenue. The best we could come up with is that Jake Gale had been alerted to Elissa's disappearance and had been heading home to join the search. He was the kind of guy who always seemed to be everywhere. Everyone knew him; he'd always put others first, help out in a crisis. Quite the pillar of the community.'

Slim had heard otherwise but chose to keep the information to himself.

'Where had he been that evening?'

'His scout hut was in Chagford, on the other side of Dartmoor. There hadn't been a club meeting that night but he spent a lot of time up there, preparing for events, things like that.'

Simon excused himself to visit the loo, and Slim leaned back, going over what first Brian and now Simon had told him.

No charges had ever been brought against Jake Gale, nor had anyone ever come forward to accuse him of indecent assault on minors in his charge. Brian's accusations came solely from what his daughter had claimed and his own deductions and theories, but the supposed five victims Brian named had all been childhood attendees of Jake Gale's scouting club. Slim had heard none of the names before, but they had all died relatively young: two as teenage suicides in the late eighties, two from substance abuse in the nineties, and a fifth had been hit by a train on the Plymouth to Dawlish line. At the time he had been unemployed and homeless.

Brian Tate had looked at the nature of each death and assumed that childhood trauma was responsible. Slim might have assumed the same, but it was nothing that would help him with his investigation, and none of it linked Jake Gale's crash with Elissa Lowescroft's disappearance.

In fact, compared to Elissa's disappearance, there was very little about Jake Gale's death that was suspicious. He had been driving much too fast late at night on a road that wasn't suitable for speed. He might have been tired, possibly even under the influence of alcohol, back when such restrictions were less strictly enforced. Slim knew from a previous case that in 1982 the wearing of seatbelts was not yet compulsory, and on the moor, at night ... Jake Gale's crash could be left out of the inquiry into Elissa's death.

Slim however, was reluctant to let it go.

As Simon had said and he had thought, it was just too much of a coincidence.

34

'SLIM? It's me. I've got something. I'm not sure how much it'll help, but it's something.'

'Anything, Don. I'm at a loss on this case. Anything might help.'

'I'm not sure this will, but you never know. I managed to uncover an extended family member of Philip Reece's, a cousin. Allegedly, in 1976, when Reece was twenty years old, he had a daughter with a woman named Sandra Rickman. They weren't married, and Sandra came from a strict Catholic family, who basically ostracised her. However, according to the cousin, Philip had hoped to marry Sandra and had been seeing the little girl in secret. He was unemployed at the time, and the parents refused to give their blessing. Philip moved down south to look for work, and eventually got a job in Rundlestone Primary. That summer, however, the little girl unfortunately died. Philip would possibly have found out during the summer, meaning that at the time of the school trip in October, he was still dealing with his grief.'

'Is this cousin still alive?'

'I don't know. I pulled this from a local newspaper article published in 1986, shortly after Philip Reece died. It was more of a personality piece, rather than one trying to give insights into Elissa's situation, and as such, I think it likely passed mostly unnoticed.'

Slim gave a thoughtful nod. 'Did it say how the little girl died?'

'She had some kind of allergic reaction. The article didn't specify, but it did say that the girl had been sickly, suffering a number of ailments as an infant, including measles, anemia, and jaundice.'

'Jaundice? That's the one that gives the skin and eyes a yellowish tint, isn't it?'

'That's right. It's quite common in babies. It's likely Philip would have witnessed it as he didn't move south until the baby was a couple of years old.'

'If Philip was still suffering from losing his child, and had seen something out on the moor that reminded him of her, his breakdown might have been triggered in some way.'

'It's possible. I'll keep digging, see if I can find anything else.'

'Thanks, Don.'

Slim hung up. Alone in his room, he sat down at the desk and began to flip through the piles of documents he had compiled. He still had no hint at a breakthrough, but he had uncovered enough new information to convince him to keep digging. The mystery, growing darker by the day, refused to let him go. Even as clouds rolled in and the coffins of long forgotten tragedies began to creak open, Slim found himself unable to look away.

If Philip had seen something in the mist that had reminded him of his recently deceased daughter, that could have triggered his sudden, unexpected breakdown.

It also might absolve him of any blame in Elissa's death.

Donald Lane had managed to provide him with a copy of the autopsy report. The file was several pages long, made up mostly of technical jargon. Slim flicked through it, looking for something that stood out as unusual.

Her cause of death was given as asphyxiation. Water had been found in her mouth and throat, but not in her lungs. There were bruises on her chest area, and on her hands. The largest impact damage was on her face, just below the left eye. Her clothes were wet, but not her socks inside her boots. The hair of various animals was found on her clothing, including horse hair, wool, and cat hair. Her fingernails were broken, and underneath was found soil, and traces of paint and lacquer. The zip on her jacket was up, but had been forced, a couple of teeth out of line as though it had been pulled shut roughly or at speed.

Slim took a deep breath and leaned back in the chair. The clues were there, indications of a rural life and education. Horse riding, helping out with family life, school art classes, and finally a school trip to the moor which had ended in tragedy.

He was just brewing more coffee when a knock came on the door. He found the elderly landlady standing outside, a Manila envelope in her hands.

'A young lady just dropped this by for you,' she said.

'Thanks.'

He took the package. The landlady closed the door, and Slim listened as her footfalls receded back downstairs.

At the desk, he opened the package. Another envelope was inside, filled with photocopies of old photographs. A handwritten note was taped to the front.

Hey, Mr. Detective, I dug out a few old family pics I thought you might like a look at. They're all copied so don't worry about returning them. I look forward to seeing you in the pub sometime. M.

The M had to be Melanie Gale. The uncomfortable warmth Slim felt around his neck was tempered by the goldmine of information. Not only had Melanie copied all the photographs, but she had annotated the reverse sides with names and dates. Being a younger and newer member of the Gale family, the information was incomplete, but it was far more than Slim might have discovered on his own.

He flicked through the pictures, feeling overawed. Some were family shots from the seventies, a powerful man labeled as William Gale standing next to a handsome young man labeled as Jake. There was one of a group of young men in pirate costumes, standing next to a decorated trailer, preparing for a carnival. Among the names were Jake, Brian, Thomas, Nathan. Thomas, Slim didn't know, but Brian had to be Brian Tate, and Nathan was Nathan Gale, Morton's dad. In every picture, Jake Gale glowed with confidence and charm, often while those around him looked caught in his shadow. Nathan Gale paled worst of all in the few pictures they were together, never a smile, his shoulders slumped. In one picture dated 1977, Jake and Nathan stood together outside a barn Slim guessed was on Gale Farm. Jake had one arm up in the air, the other around Nathan's shoulders. Nathan was looking away from the camera, his eyes downcast, as though reluctant to have his picture taken.

Having so recently looked into Jake Gale's car crash, Slim found it hard to move past the photographs of Aaron's father, but they were only a fraction of the pictures Melanie had prepared. More showed groups of local children at play around the farm, or on horseback, walking on the moor. Among them were Elissa, Morton, Ginny, and there was even one of Victoria at a village fete, grinning as she presided over a stall of honey and jam. Still more were landscapes of Dartmoor, Lydford Gorge, Brent Tor, St Michael's church, a couple of the local school, and then one Slim found it hard to look away from.

The road was the one outside the little primary school from which the children had departed. Twelve children stood beside a coach, partly obscuring the moniker Greg's Coaches, an underside door lifted, school bags, as well as rolled picnic mats, and even a couple of shovels, visible inside. Nearby stood George Stockwood, Philip Reece, Margaret Leddon, and the driver, leaning back with an awkward grin on his face and a cigarette in one hand as though trying to get out of shot.

Everyone looked happy, even the teachers. Everyone, that is, except Elissa, who was looking away from the camera, across towards the teachers, with a stony and sour expression on her face.

35

Whatever had happened, Slim felt certain it had been planned by Elissa but had gone wrong. He needed to talk to Robina again, get a clearer picture of Elissa's personality, but he had to tread carefully. The pictures Melanie had given him had offered a theory which made him uncomfortable. When the time came that he would have to push further, he wasn't sure how he would broach the subject. For now, though, he had to keep his ideas to himself.

He went to see Robina. She had set out some cakes and biscuits on a little patio to enjoy the unseasonably warm afternoon. Slim felt a little uncomfortable with the subject matter, so spent a few minutes talking pointlessly about the weather and the moorland while Robina prepared and poured the coffee.

'I know this is a strange request, but do you have any more school books of Elissa's?' Slim asked as he sipped at some fairly decent coffee.

'I'll have a look up in the loft later,' she said.

'And any photographs of Elissa and your family. I know

this is hard for you, but I'm still building up a picture of what happened. Was Elissa into arts and crafts?'

'Oh, yes,' Robina said. 'It was probably her favourite subject after … well, riding horses.'

'I have one more question. Did she take much time off school? Like, was she often sick?'

'Almost never.'

'Any days off that September term?'

Robina frowned. 'It's tough to remember so long ago … but I imagine if there had been, I'd be more likely to remember it. So, I'd say no.'

'That's fine. I just wondered. And how was she with you, if you don't mind me asking? I mean, strong-willed, meek, that kind of thing.'

Robina gave a wistful smile. 'Oh, she knew everything, did Elissa. Was always telling me I was wrong, should do things differently. Wouldn't let anyone tell her what to do. She wasn't a bad girl, though. Just something of a know it all. I think it came from being so good with the horses at such a young age. She'd never had any bad falls, never had one misbehave. That can break a young rider and I was always so fearful of it happening, but Elissa was too good with them, a total natural. It gave her confidence in everything.'

Slim found it hard to stay focused as Robina began to wax lyrical about the merits of horse riding. He waited for Robina to pause, then said, 'Did Elissa ever go to the classes run by Jake Gale?'

The mood in the room palpably changed. Robina's smile dropped and she began to play with a frayed tassel on the edge of the sofa.

'She went a few times,' Robina said at last. 'I wasn't too happy about it, though.'

'Any particular reason?'

Robina shook her head without looking up. 'Jake Gale was….'

Slim wanted to hear her back up Brian Tate's claims, but she trailed off, shaking her head. Then, with a sigh, she added, 'He wasn't everyone's cup of tea, that was all.'

'I hear he was something of a pillar of the community.'

Robina relaxed, like a fish let off the hook. 'He was that, I suppose. William Gale was still running the farm in those days so Jake had the time to get involved in the local community. He was always organising things, running events.'

'But he would have been quite young at the time?'

'Early thirties, I suppose,' Robina said, when Slim felt she could have told him exactly how old Jake Gale had been at the time of her daughter's death.

'I heard that he died following a car accident the same night Elissa died,' Slim said. 'It's a terrible coincidence, having two tragedies on the same night like that. Although I gather his crash was somewhat overshadowed by the search for Elissa, and that he didn't die until some weeks later.'

Robina shifted uncomfortably. Slim regretted his line of thought, but her reaction was what he had expected.

'I'm not sure what you're implying,' Robina said.

'The police, I believe, felt the two events tragic but entirely separate, although I heard a rumour that Jake Gale might have been speeding home in order to join the search and had lost control.'

'That would have been like Jake.' Robina looked away as she answered, Slim studying her eyes, the way her hands fidgeted in her lap. 'That was exactly the kind of thing Jake Gale would have done. He was always one to look out for the community.'

36

THE HISTORY SECTIONS of the local libraries in Tavistock and Okehampton offered up a couple of picture books on the local community, but Slim struck gold when he came across a social media page of local photographs and discovered it was run by Debbie Gladstone, the curt but elegant older woman whom he had met at the WI meeting. He found her address listed on the page, then drove over to see her unannounced, parking a little way up the road from her house.

She lived in a beautiful three-storey stone building called Brentor Grange, reached by a long sweeping driveway and surrounded by professionally manicured gardens. Slim couldn't imagine living somewhere so expansive yet graceful; he felt more empathy with the line of converted stables half hidden behind a privet hedge. That a pack of Dobermans didn't appear to savage him before he reached the front door was a bonus, that no alarm went off as he rang the doorbell was another, and that Debbie actually answered the door was a third.

'Yes, can I help you? Oh, it's John Hardy, isn't it? I

remember you from the meeting the other week. So, you're still around?'

Her tone had softened somewhat, but still held an edge of suspicion.

'I'm sorry to stop by unannounced.' He pulled the ancient Nokia—which he had switched off—out of his pocket and held it up. 'I forgot to charge my phone. I'm in the wrong generation.'

Debbie's frostiness melted just a little. 'You and me both.'

'I came across your web page. The local photographs?'

'Oh, yes. Something of a retirement hobby.'

'I was wondering if I could take a look at what photos you have from the late seventies up to 1982. There were a couple of events that year that I have a particular interest in.'

Debbie's frostiness melted just a little more. 'Sure, come in. Would you like a cup of tea? I just made a pot.'

Slim didn't, but he gave her his best smile and said, 'That would be very kind. Thank you.'

It seemed that Debbie just took a little time to thaw. Once Slim was sitting down at the table and Debbie was arranging both a laptop with a digital database and a box of old photographs in front of him, she began to relax her guard, talking with increasing freedom about both her hobby and her past. Slim didn't even need to ask as she began to recite her own recollections of the time of Elissa's disappearance and death.

'I am—or was—a corporate lawyer,' she said. 'My own children were in secondary school at the time, and I was actually up working in London that week. I remember coming home on the Saturday morning, and she had just been found. My husband—he passed a few years ago— had joined the search.'

'That must have been harrowing.'

'He had just got home when I arrived. He was sitting at the table, still wearing his boots. There was mud all over the floor and I remember starting to feel angry until I saw the look in his eyes. He was in the group that found her.'

'In the stream?'

'Just back from the water. She was lying face down in a patch of marshy ground. He told me later that when he first saw her in the light of the torch, he felt like the world had ended. He told me that night that he knew there was no god. No god could ever be so cruel.'

'Did they touch the body? Move it in any way?'

'I only know what he said. He told me that he went forward to check, but someone called out that she was definitely dead, that it was a crime scene. They waited for the police after that.'

'Can you remember who was with him?'

Debbie frowned. 'He told me once. There was him, Steven something-or-other who worked at the timber mill in Tavistock, James Greg, ah, Robert …. Cole, that was it —who lived over in Stourton, and …' She frowned again, tapping her fingers on the tabletop. 'That was it. Nathan Gale.'

Slim gave a slow nod. 'And do you remember anything else that your husband told you? You said someone claimed she was definitely dead.'

'I imagine it was probably obvious from looking at her.'

'I'm sure. Could it have been Nathan Gale?'

Debbie gave a slow smile. 'John, you're a detective, I am—was—a lawyer. I know how these things work. I don't remember if my husband said it was Nathan Gale or said those words or not, but your question tells me you believe Nathan Gale might have been involved in Elissa's murder.'

There was no point in lying to a lawyer, corporate or otherwise.

'Yes, I do,' Slim said. 'I have a number of theories. One is that Elissa was involved in an elaborate prank, one which involved her running off and laying low for a while. She knew the area well, even in the fog, and I believe she might have gone as far as Gale Farm, where she ran into Nathan Gale. Something happened then that left her dead. Nathan could have taken her body to the moor, then later, during the search, subtly directed his group to where she was found.'

Debbie gave Slim an approving nod. 'That's quite some theory. What evidence do you have?'

Slim gave a grim smile. 'None. Only a timeframe that fits.'

'That's a start. But why would Elissa go up to Gale Farm? I know the area well. Going across the moor to St. Michael's church or looping around back to the car park would have been quicker.'

'You know about Philip Reece?'

'I've read the articles, heard the rumours, like everyone else.'

'And what do you make of it?'

'You're the detective, not me.'

She left the sentence hanging, playing Slim's own trick back at him. And it worked. He found words he should have kept to himself lining up on his tongue.

'I believe she panicked. Whatever Reece saw out there on the moor, Elissa saw it too. She fled, heading northeast, and came to the lane that leads around to Gale Farm. She went there looking for help, but ran into Nathan Gale. He was a known drunk and a thug. If she did run into him, things could have ended badly for her.'

He looked across the table, but Debbie was staring at the tabletop.

'Nathan's dead,' she said, not looking up. 'He can't answer your questions.'

'If I can find someone to confirm he was home at Gale Farm that day—'

'You won't.'

'But—'

Debbie stood up and walked towards the kitchen. 'I need a drink,' she said. 'Will you join me?'

'Not unless you want me to drink everything you have and then pass out on your floor. If you have coffee, I would prefer it.'

Debbie didn't look back. 'I want you to leave Nathan Gale out of whatever investigation you're conducting,' she said. 'He was screwed from the day he was born into that godforsaken family. The poor cousin with the gambler father who threw everything they had away. He didn't have a chance.'

Slim shifted in his seat. 'You can give him an alibi, can't you?'

Debbie didn't look back at him. Her shoulders shifted, and Slim realised she was crying.

'Yes,' she said.

37

'I met him when he came around for some advice one day,' Debbie said, sitting at the table, a glass of wine tilted at such an angle Slim felt sure it would spill at any moment. 'He'd been in a bar fight, heard I was a lawyer, even if he didn't know what branch of law I practiced.' She sighed. 'At first I didn't like him either.'

'You had an affair?'

Debbie lifted a finger to object, then threw her hands up in the air.

'We might as well call a spade a spade. I prefer fling. It was a physical thing. He was hard to like. I suppose I saw him as a project. His cousin Jake was the local heartthrob, the heir to the empire, and Nathan was the table scraps, drinking and fighting himself into oblivion. Rarely have I met someone so full of resentment, but behind it all there was a good man. At least I thought so. I hoped so. In the end, he got away from me, too.'

'And the night Elissa died?'

'We were at a hotel in Exeter. He was officially off

looking for work, but I don't think his wife and son cared, so long as he was out of the picture.'

'But he was back for the search?'

Debbie shook her head and sighed. 'We … quarrelled. It was never far away with Nathan, but he had no hold over me. We fought a lot, and it was often rough, but he never laid a hand on me. That night was probably the closest he ever came. I kicked him out of the room, sent him on his way. He caught a bus down to Tavistock, arrived home just as the search was getting underway.'

'Did you never fear he would reveal your affair?'

Debbie spread her hands. 'In your words, "a drunk and a thug" versus a corporate lawyer? Who would believe him?'

Slim just nodded. 'Right.'

'What I do know is that he wasn't at Gale Farm at the time he needed to be to fit your theory of Elissa's murder. He was in bed with me. That rules him out.'

'If you're telling the truth.'

'Unless you have evidence to prove otherwise, we'll have to assume I am for now. What else do you have, John?'

Slim took a sip of tepid coffee. 'Why don't we have a look at those photographs?'

He left Debbie's house a couple of hours later, feeling both that he'd made some headway while sailing into a headwind at the same time, and now he was spinning around, backtracking, returning to where he'd begun.

He had a couple of missed calls on his phone: one from Kay and another from an unrecognised number. Kay didn't answer when he returned the call, so he tried the latter, getting an automated system for the HM Prison Service.

Morton. He called the prison, but it was out of hours to contact prisoners, so he resolved to call back tomorrow.

He went back to the B&B. He had taken pictures of many of those Debbie had shown him, so he uploaded the data from his camera to his laptop and scrolled through them while looking over the others he had assembled at the same time.

Debbie claimed that she received photos from local people on an almost daily basis. Usually scanned but sometimes in print, they often came from people clearing out their lofts and cupboards. Most that she posted online dated back a hundred years or more and usually depicted farming landscapes, old houses, or family groups. She had a lot of more personal ones too, but posted few publicly out of respect for those shown in them. In addition, many were blurry, poorly lit, or of little interest.

'There are a few morbid types, though,' she had told him.

She had several photos that Slim would describe as crime scenes, related to the search for Elissa Lowescroft. One showed the start of the search effort, a few dozen people gathered in the dusky car park near St. Michael's church, gathering into groups ready to head out onto the moor. Slim recognised no one; most had their backs turned or were looking away. On the back Debbie had labeled a few of them, though: Craig Jones, Robert Cole, Arthur Smith, and others. Few were names Slim recognised. The photographs had allegedly been taken by William Gale and passed to Debbie some years back by his late wife, Ethel.

There were also some photos taken after the search had concluded. An ambulance stood in the car park, alongside three police cars parked haphazardly, a bus, several other cars. People had returned from the moor, and appeared dazed and bedraggled in the flash of the camera. Finally, here were some faces Slim recognised from old photos: Robina Lowescroft, Nathan Gale, Ms. Leddon, James Greg, a few more whose names he couldn't remember.

And there, standing to the side in one photo, was a much younger, but clearly recognisable Brian Tate.

Looking back at the pictures on his laptop screen, Slim stared at the man for a long time. The search had ended early in the morning after Elissa's disappearance, meaning there would have been time for Brian to come across the moor from Postbridge following Jake Gale's accident, but would he have done? He had told Slim he had not heard about the disappearance until after Elissa's body had been found, but here he was, photographed at the location.

Slim pressed his hands against his temples. It was a knot of unholy proportions. Yet, through the murk, things were beginning to take on a little shape.

He moved most of the photos aside and pulled out two that had caught his interest before his meeting with Debbie Gladstone.

One showed a smiling Jake Gale with his arm around an attractive girl who looked at the camera with her head tilted sideways, almost shy. It was dated 1971. The other was a family group picture dated 1981, a man and woman, both with awkward, eighties hair, alongside two young girls, one tall and gangly, the other shorter, already a little overweight for her age.

Ten years apart, hair different and clearly older but the tilt of her head made her identifiable, the woman in both pictures was the same.

Robina Lowescroft.

And just from looking at the differences between the two girls, and by estimating their ages, Slim felt certain that Elissa didn't belong to the man Robina had married, but instead to the man with whom she had been in a relationship several years before: Jake Gale.

38

ANDY.

So caught up in the web of local intrigue spun around the truth about Elissa Lowescroft's death, Slim had often found Andy and the mystery of the toy bears slipping from his mind. Now, as he stared at a grainy picture of Elissa holding up a junior level showjumping trophy with a beaming smile on her face, another puzzle piece fell into place.

Her horse stood beside her, head turned away from the camera as though put off by the attention. Slim couldn't even guess at the breed: he could differentiate them only by size and colour. But the object tied to the front part of the saddle—the pommel, he believed it was called—was far more familiar.

A little teddy bear, secured at a crooked angle, its head tilted drunkenly towards the camera.

And even though the picture was black and white, Slim felt certain the real life bear was blue.

So, the bear made sense. Why Andy, was another matter, but when Audrey emailed him an exhaustive list of everyone she could think of that Andy had interacted with over the last six months prior to the commencement of his ritual, at least it gave him another lead.

It was drudge work, though. The list went from doctors down to family members, neighbours, local shop owners, even delivery people. And while Slim wished he had time to investigate such leads as "the man from Parcel World who brings the cat food every other Tuesday", it would take considerable time to get through the list.

The phone call he received from Morton Gale offered another, stronger lead.

'I don't know what to say other than that I appreciate it,' Morton told him. I got a parole hearing for December. I could be out for Christmas. If so, I'll buy you a pint.'

'I'll settle for a coffee. But good luck.'

Morton explained that he had spoken with his mother, and she had agreed to speak to Slim. So that afternoon Slim drove over to a care home on the outskirts of Plymouth.

From the outside the place was not much to look at, barely larger than a family home, and it turned out to only have six residents. After signing in at a reception desk, a staff member led him to a pretty rear conservatory overlooking a bland rectangle of neatly cut grass, the garden's only feature a bird table just outside the window.

Linda Gale, Morton's mother, was a wiry old thing who looked at least ninety. She was waiting for him in a wicker chair, with a view of the bird table, where a pair of sparrows were currently fussing over a flat pyramid of sunflower seeds.

'Grew those in the garden this year,' Linda said, lifting a hooked arthritic finger. 'They're going to get fat, stuffing themselves like this.'

'Thank you for agreeing to meet me,' Slim said.

'You're the detective the boy was talking about,' Linda said. Her voice was weak and gravelly, as though it was a struggle to speak. Slim got the impression she was only partly talking to him, her words as much for herself.

'I'm a private investigator,' he said. 'I'm investigating the death of one of Morton's classmates in 1982.'

'Elissa, yes, the boy said,' Linda said. 'Such a terrible thing. She was a nice girl, always looked out for my Morton, even when no one else wanted anything to do with him.'

Slim wasn't sure what to say. Linda was still staring at the bird table as though it were a gateway to a world long left behind.

'He was never popular,' Linda said with a gentle sigh. 'And after she died, it got even harder. She was his only real friend.'

'How do you think she died?'

'Oh, drowned on the moor, like the coroner said. No reason to doubt it. All this fuss about people going mad and ghostly children, that's just Dartmoor playing with people's minds. It can do that.'

'You don't believe there was any foul play?'

'No, I can't imagine it. It was a tragedy. They happen.'

Slim paused. She spoke with such conviction that for a moment he thought she might be right. Perhaps he had been chasing ghosts all this time.

'You know, I came up with a theory that your ex-husband was involved,' Slim said. 'I've since found evidence that my theory was wrong.'

For the first time, Linda turned to look at him, a sudden brightness in her eyes which made him nervous.

'The drink got him in the end,' she said at last. 'It was a shame, but he never had a chance. I thought I could … guide him, but I was wrong.'

'I heard he was … violent,' Slim said.

'He could be, yes. It was always the drink, though. And he'd had to fight his entire life. It was all he knew. And how would you like it living off your own family's crumbs?'

'I don't understand.'

'Nathan's dad blew everything, gambled it away. After he died, William let him stay in the old cottage on the farm in exchange for a bit of work. Barely a day went past when they didn't threaten to pull it all out from under him. He dreamed of having the last laugh, but he never did. Probably the happiest I've ever seen him was the day Jake died.'

'Jake? His cousin?'

'Yes, that's right. What an uppity little so and so he was. Didn't care he was married, had that nice little boy. He was off with every woman who'd have him in a five-mile radius. The only reason Nathan started playing around was because he was trying to prove something.'

Slim decided not to mention Debbie Gladstone. 'Nathan was playing around?'

'He had a couple of flings, I know that. I was twelve years his senior, no oil painting even then. He did right and married me when he got me pregnant with Morton, and we were happy at first, but nothing was good enough for Nathan. He wanted what Jake had and couldn't have it. And it drove him into the ground. But for Jake's accident, he'd have drunk himself to death ten years earlier.'

'Jake's death meant he took over the running of the farm?'

'Only for a while. William did most of it, him and that wretched Brian Tate. And Nathan had the drink holding him back. William gradually brought in more help, and in the end, Nathan was back where he started, drinking himself to death in that gloomy, damp-ridden little cottage.'

'You mentioned Brian Tate? I gather you weren't fond of him.'

Linda wrinkled her nose. 'He was Jake's little friend,' she said with a bitter sneer. 'They were best mates and all that, and their favorite pastime was making Nathan's life a misery. I remember this one time they caught him stealing a few eggs. It was my birthday the next day and the dumb drunken fool had decided to make me a cake. Jake and Brian caught him red-handed. They dragged him behind the chicken shed and they absolutely hammered him. My present that year from the good old Gale family was a husband with two black eyes. To be honest, I wasn't sorry to see the back of Jake Gale either. The only downside was that Brian Tate wasn't in the car with him.'

Slim sipped a cup of tea a staff member had brought him while Linda stared out of the window.

'I hear you helped my lad get a parole hearing,' Linda said, turning to watch the birds.

'I asked for a favour,' Slim said. 'The rest is up to him.'

'He's not a bad lad,' Linda said. 'He just got involved with the wrong people. You know, he told me it happened because he was sticking up for someone about to get it worse?'

'I hope he can come out to a better life,' Slim said.

'And he can take care of me. It's the Gales paying for this,' she said. 'Not exactly five-star, though, is it? Better than nothing. Old William always felt an obligation to Nathan, but what I wouldn't do to be rid of that family for good.'

'Can I ask you one more thing? Is it possible that Jake Gale had any illegitimate children?'

Linda let out a bitter laugh. 'Any? Half of North Devon probably sprang from his rutting loins.'

'What about Elissa Lowescroft?'

'Oh, I'm not sure. I know he was with Robina Northcott for a while, but I couldn't say.'

'Northcott?'

'Maiden name. She wasn't no oil painting either, but neither was Roger Lowescroft. They were good together though, so happy.'

'So, you don't think Elissa was Jake's daughter?'

'It's possible, I suppose. We always wondered about Ginny Tate, and that sickly Leddon girl, didn't have no dad anyone knew of, although I think she might have moved down from elsewhere, can't remember well now—'

Slim's ears were ringing. The revelation that Ginny Tate might have been the daughter of Brian Tate's best friend was one thing, but there was more.

'What Leddon girl?'

'Maggie Leddon's girl. Didn't go to the local school. She was always too sick.'

39

SHE WAS SCRITCHING at Morton this morning for not washing his hands. Like, he soon won't have any hands left.

Slim looked over the lines of text Kay had deciphered from the maths book. Little made much sense, but he felt like he was close to a breakthrough. Robina had found him two more, from September and October, 1982, and he had sent both to Kay for analysis.

I saw her again the other day when I went to Okehampton with Dad. Why doesn't she come here?

He put Kay's notes away and turned back to the photographs.

Linda had raised more questions instead of offering answers. Where she had poured water on his growing flames of suspicion, a spark still flickered. He stared at the pictures of Elissa Lowescroft and Jake Gale and tried to see how they weren't related in some way. And if they were related, might Jake have known?

Perhaps Robina had been in denial. Perhaps her dislike of Elissa attending Jake's classes had been to avoid them running into each other, seeing the truth face to face. Or maybe Ginny Tate's claims had been true, and Robina had been seeking to avoid a horrifying situation becoming worse.

His phone rang. Donald Lane.

'Slim, I found something you might find interesting. I'm emailing over some pictures. Have you got your computer handy?'

'Right here, Don.'

'All right, sending them over.'

'What are they?'

'Photos from the scene of Jake Gale's car crash. I managed to find an old police report. At first it was treated as suspicious due to the nature and timing of the event, although later it was classified as an accident. There were extensive photos taken the morning after. I thought you might like a look.'

'Thanks, Don, I would. While I've got you on the line, can I ask you to see what you can find regarding Margaret Leddon, Elissa's teacher at the time of her death? Anything about her family, her career. I heard that she might have lived in one of the cottages on the main road that passes Brent Tor, that are now holiday lets. If she's still alive, I'd love to talk to her.'

'Sure. I'll see what I can do.'

Slim hung up, then opened the email Don had sent. It contained an attachment with about thirty photographs of the aftermath of Jake Gale's accident.

Slim had no specific skills when it came to car crash analysis, but his basic observation was that the car had impacted at a significant speed. The entire front of the car was buckled, the bonnet popped up, the front wheels embedded into the ground, the tyres burst.

There were no pictures of Jake or Aaron, but there were some from several angles, close ups, distance shots,

shots of tyre marks in the ground. Bad weather had left the area marshy and rescue vehicles had contaminated the scene by leaving a crisscrossing of additional tyre treads. Slim stared at a photo taken from the roadside showing the car smashed into the rocky outcrop at a right angle from the road, and frowned.

He pulled out his phone and called Simon Clifford.

'Hey, Slim. What can I do for you?'

'Was it ever theorised that Jake Gale might have been driving away from Brent Tor at the time of his accident, rather than returning, as people have claimed?'

Simon chuckled. 'So, you noticed the tyre marks too?'

'A friend found me some pictures of the scene taken the morning after. There's a distinct disturbance of turf in an arc by the roadside that angles from north to south. If he had been coming from the southwest, it would have been angled the opposite way. Assuming that's the mark where Jake Gale came off the road.'

'You could be right. No tyre tread analysis was done, and a couple of hours after the pictures were taken, there was a heavy thunderstorm that made them unusable. I put it to a retired policeman once, who claimed the tracks could have been caused by a squad car. In the end, when nothing criminal was ever linked to Jake Gale or his crash, it was forgotten about.'

'It should never have been,' Slim said, remembering Brian Tate's words, that Jake had been travelling home. 'Because if he was going away from Brent Tor instead of coming back … it changes everything.'

40

THAT BRIAN TATE, seemingly so stoically honest, could have lied to him was one thing, but that Jake Gale could have been doing the opposite of what had been claimed was another.

Rather than rushing back to Brent Tor to assist in the search for the missing Elissa, Jake Gale could have been driving away from Brent Tor, at speed, in the middle of the night.

And Brian Tate had lied about it.

Why?

There was one solid reason, although again it was little more than speculation.

Despite what he had told Slim, claiming they weren't close, Linda believed Brian and Jake had been best friends. The pictures Slim had seen of them together backed that up. But could it have been even more than that, that Brian had been in awe of his friend, the son of the biggest local landowner, and even after everything had gone down, despite serious allegations against him, Brian had tried to protect Jake's reputation, by claiming he was heroically returning to help find a missing girl, rather than running away?

Slim felt a sick feeling in his stomach. He looked through his piles of notes until he found the autopsy report for Elissa's death.

Bruising on her face, chest and stomach, suggested as consistent with landing on rocks after tripping up.

Simon Clifford agreed to a walk on the moor the next day, considering it was a fine, sunny morning. Slim picked him up in Tavistock, then drove back across the moor, passed St. Michael's church, and up the dead-end road to the point where it ended. He parked on the verge and together they headed down the hill to Elissa's monument.

Another little blue teddy bear sat on the top, freshly made. Slim smiled, then as an afterthought while Simon was wandering about further up the stream, reached into his pocket and pulled out the poor attempt of his own, placing it on top of the monument, still in the little bag. Coaker's chip was still inside, but whether it would still be charged, several days after Slim's failed attempt to place it at Brian Tate's door, he didn't know. It was symbolic of the shambles his investigation had become, but it was a last throw of the dice, and sometimes your numbers came up.

Simon, unawares, had walked a little way up the slope from the stream. He stopped next to a triangular lump of granite sticking out from among tufts of grass. Lichen covered one side, the one facing away from the sun.

'Right here,' Simon told him, squatting down. 'She was found right here, lying this way, facing sideways across the slope.'

'And there were no tracks, indicating which way she had come?'

'The ground was marshy, and there were a lot of people out looking for her. Impossible to decide which tracks were hers.'

'What about hoof prints?'

'Several people had gone out on horseback, so they could cover more ground.'

'From the angle it looks like she was heading downhill.'

'That's what was theorised, yes.'

'It was raining that night?'

'Yes.'

'Do you know what time the rain started?'

Simon smiled and shrugged. 'Slim ... I ... it was a long time ago. I believe it was foggy through the evening, turning into drizzle later. You'd need to check with the Met Office.'

Slim nodded, then squatted and ran a hand through the grass. 'Was it windy?'

'I don't recall.'

'So, we could suggest she was heading for lower ground, where she knew there would be trees to offer shelter.'

'I would presume so.'

'That's what I would do. That's what we were trained to do in the Armed Forces. Find cover, reduce lines of sight.'

'Right.'

Slim pointed upslope. 'Let's walk upslope a little.'

Simon agreed, and they headed uphill, picking their way through rocks protruding from the grass. A few times Slim nearly tripped on smaller buried rocks, but the slope was flat enough for him to correct himself without alarm.

When he reached a viewing spot, he paused to wait for Simon to catch up. 'Are you all right?'

Simon smiled. 'I'm seventy-five, and it's like a minefield.'

'How about we run back down?'

'Not a chance.'

'Even in daylight?'

'No.'

Slim sat down on a rock and pulled a flask of coffee out of the rucksack he was carrying. He offered a spare cup to Simon who gratefully took it and sat on a rock nearby.

'So, on a clear day, we couldn't run down that hillside,' Slim said. 'I think it's safe to assume that Elissa wouldn't have, not at night, in the dark, in the rain.'

'I think you knew that already.'

'I did. Tell me, do you know if Brian Tate had a cat?'

41

SLIM REMEMBERED something Robina had said on his first visit. Elissa had loved all animals. She had even loved cats, despite an allergy.

Both horse and cat hair had been found on her clothing. The horse hair was explainable for a lover of horses, the cat hair less so.

Of course, Slim would be foolish to read too much into it. Cats were everywhere in the countryside, and Elissa could have picked up the hairs off a classmate.

The bruising on her chest was more significant. It could easily have been caused by a fall, but it was also possibly due to an ongoing repeated action.

Being bumped up and down, for example.

The problem Slim had was proving anything. He had already asked Simon if any physical evidence from Elissa's post-mortem examination had been saved, but the old reporter had just shook his head.

'This is Devon and Cornwall Police, not the Met,' he said. 'One of the smallest forces in the country. They don't have the resources to store every last thing, especially not on closed cases.'

'So I have little chance of proving anything with forensics,' Slim said.

'I'd say none.'

It would come down to compelling circumstantial evidence, or a confession, neither of which Slim felt particularly optimistic about. And while he had one or two theories, he was yet to come up with anything he could explain with confidence.

All he felt certain of was that Elissa had died off the moor, and that someone had placed her back on the moor after her death, later joining the search party as a cover. With people coming and going in the dark, it would be impossible to tell who had come later.

Except perhaps by looking at the photographs he had seen at Debbie's.

Brian Tate, for example. The old hunt master had placed himself at the scene of Jake Gale's accident, something verifiable from police records, but was later seen in the photographs of the car park at Brent Tor shortly after Elissa's discovery.

The problem with using the photographs as evidence was that they were only a snapshot. They didn't show everyone, they didn't show all the vehicles present at the start and the end of the search. There would have been others, maybe only shown in one, or maybe in none. As evidence, it was paper thin.

Brian Tate, however, was a good place to start.

'If I can just cross you off the list,' Slim muttered to himself. 'And if I can't … well. We'll see where that road ends.'

Sitting alone in a café in Tavistock, he went over what he knew; what were as close to facts as he could get.

Elissa had gone missing on Dartmoor at around 3pm on Friday the 22nd of October. Her body had been found during an extensive search on the moor in the early hours of Saturday the 23rd, less than five hundred yards from where she had last been seen. The autopsy report gave her death as asphyxiation, caused by being knocked unconscious and falling in water. Her clothes were wet. She had horse and cat hair on her clothing, bruising on her chest, soil and paint under her fingernails.

The report claimed that due to the state of digestion of the contents of her stomach, she had been alive for up to six hours after her disappearance.

While Elissa had still been missing, ten miles across the moor at Postbridge, Jake Gale had crashed his car in what would later prove a fatal crash. A four-year-old Aaron Gale had been in the back but survived. The crash was reported to the police by Brian Tate, who had not told the police that he had been out on the road, waiting for Jake's car.

It was claimed Jake had been driving southwest, back towards Brent Tor, but tyre marks suggested he could have been driving northeast, away from the area.

At one time, Jake Gale had been in a relationship with Robina Northcott, and Elissa bore a striking resemblance to Jake.

Slim sighed, making abstract circles with a pen on a paper napkin. He felt like he was getting nowhere.

He turned to his notes on Elissa's cause of death.

The coroner's report claimed accidental. The evidence fit, but it was an easy win, except for the six-hour period in which Elissa might still have been alive.

Slim felt certain that she had not died on the moor.

Nathan Gale, a local thug and drunk, had an alibi, if Debbie Gladstone were to be believed.

There had been no investigation of sexual assault, and

there had been no marks to suggest any kind of struggle. The only blunt trauma wounds were consistent with a fall.

Slim had rested a lot of his suspicions on the possibility that Elissa had been murdered, but now he felt certain that her death had been accidental. In order to avoid ostracism or stigma, she had been placed on the moor and left for the search party to find.

Slim felt certain he knew the answer. He finished his coffee, then went outside to call Robina.

'It had been lined up for late November,' Robina said, sitting across from Slim at her dining table. 'Gordon had been offered a transfer to Norfolk. Better position, much better money. The company was going to assist financially with the move, too. Elissa knew and wasn't particularly happy about it at first, but we had already identified a couple of riding stables and she had come around to the idea, particularly when she learned that an Olympic medalist also practiced at one of them.'

'Was your planned move common knowledge?'

'Well, we had told the school and a few neighbours, so I suppose that yes, it was.'

'How did Elissa feel about leaving her friends?'

'Well, like any other child her age, she was sad about it, but she would have been fine.' Robina sniffed, then pulled a tissue from a box and dabbed at her eye. 'After her death it all fell through. We didn't have the heart to move anymore.'

Slim nodded. 'I'm sorry for how things worked out.'

After leaving Robina's place, Slim couldn't shake a sense of dejection as he walked back through the village to where he had intentionally left his car some distance away. He climbed over a stile into a field bordering the moorland and walked a little way up a gentle rise until he could see St. Michael's church rising on the tor in the distance.

Not for the first time, he considered walking away. Perhaps he was wrong, and in a sudden panic Elissa had decided to run down the hillside in the dark, tripping up, bruising herself, and knocking herself unconscious, finally suffocating in the marshy ground a little up the hill from the river.

But he didn't think so.

However, without some solid evidence, he couldn't prove anything.

Jake Gale's wife had died some years ago. And William Gale, the patriarch of the family, was in a care home in Tavistock, allegedly suffering from dementia, just a couple of years shy of his one hundredth birthday. If there were family secrets to be talked out of the old man, Slim felt unsure he'd get them with any sense of clarity, and while he'd lowered his moral code enough times in the past to question people he considered vulnerable, he found himself reluctant.

Instead, he decided to take a step back, look at the wider picture. He had gone deep into the theory that Jake Gale was somehow involved, but the only person who might know anything was Brian Tate. Slim felt certain Brian wasn't going to offer anything else voluntarily, and while he knew Brian was lying, he couldn't prove it.

He went back to the car and pulled out his notes. He looked at the list of children in Elissa's class. There were still a couple left whom he had failed to identify. Maybe

Debbie Gladstone could help. He was just about to call her when his phone rang.

Kay Skelton.

'Kay? Did you find anything on those new books?'

'Yes, I did.' Kay sounded frantic. 'But there's more, Slim. Something that could be important. Something that literally flips things on their head.'

42

SLIM DROVE BACK to the B&B, went up to his room and opened up his laptop. Then, when he saw the messages appear, he called Kay back.

I saw her again when Dad went over there to mend a fence. I was reading in the car. I saw her looking out of the window. Why doesn't she go to school?

Two days later: *I took Penelope on our Brentor loop yesterday. I saw her in the window. She's about our age. She was wearing something over her mouth, like a mask.*

And then, the following day: *I don't think she's allowed to go to school.*

There was more, but Slim needed to take it piece by piece. He took a deep breath, made a coffee from the filter machine in his room, then called Victoria Aldridge on a mobile number she had given him.

'Hey, Slim. What can I do for you?'

'Sorry to call without warning, Victoria. I just wanted to ask you a few follow-up questions, if you don't mind.'

'I'm pretty sure I've told you everything, but ask away.'

'During your time at the school, what were your impressions of Ginny Tate?'

'Ginny? Well, I told you before. She was always nice to me. Only when we were alone, though. Never when there were others around. I think she felt sorry for me not having any friends.'

'And what about Elissa?'

'I've told you all this, before, Slim.'

'I know. Tell me again, please.'

'She was standoffish, unfriendly. To be honest, she mostly just ignored me. I don't think she was all that interested in me. I wasn't into horses, you see.'

'And can you remember how they behaved towards Ms. Leddon?'

'The teacher?'

'Yes.'

'Oh, they didn't like her at all. But while Elissa was all full of backchat, Ginny would suck up to her. It was pretty obvious to everyone but Ms. Leddon fell for it.'

'So neither liked her?'

'Not at all. To be honest, she wasn't very likeable. You got the feeling she didn't care about us all that much, that she was going through the motions. I was only there a couple of months, but she was late a lot, went home early quite often, and sometimes we'd even get a substitute teacher. But she never looked sick or anything when she came back.'

Slim nodded. 'Thank you. I have one last question. Can you remember who had a horse called Penelope?'

'Oh, that would have been Elissa.'

Slim grimaced. 'Thanks, Victoria. That's great.'

He groaned as he ended the call and put his Nokia down on the desk. Victoria had contradicted what Kay had told him, while giving him a new lead at the same time.

He headed up to the moors for a walk. Unable to let anything go, however, he found himself sitting on the grassy slope below St. Michael's church, staring out across the wilds of Dartmoor. With one hand he pulled up tufts of grass, tossing the blades up into the air for the wind to catch.

Down in the river valley a short distance to the north, a little girl had played a prank and ended up dead.

He turned, looking out across the moor towards Postbridge. Hidden behind distant hills, the way was nevertheless relatively flat, perhaps an easy horse ride for someone who knew the area. But in poor weather or at night?

Slim shook his head. Impossible.

Maybe.

He was about to get up and leave when he spotted a couple walking around the base of Brent Tor, three dogs running back and forth around them.

Aaron and Melanie Gale.

Slim started to get up, then stopped and settled back down. He was done disturbing people, upending their lives in pursuit of ghosts. Let them have their time.

He shifted, looking further west and north, towards Liftondown and Bratton Clovelly. It was a beautiful part of the world, yet desolate, haunting, the kind of place that sunk its teeth in and held on.

Perhaps he should leave, stand up and walk away—

'Slim?'

Yet the mysteries had a way of holding on to him, as though they were living, breathing things, refusing to let him go.

'Slim? Is that you?'

They were standing just down the slope, Melanie and Aaron, the dogs playing in the grass further down. He looked up.

'Just enjoying the view.'

'Have you figured out your mystery yet?' Aaron asked. •

There it was, unintentional perhaps, just a hint of condescension. That assumption that Slim was chasing ghosts, searching for conspiracies, hunting secrets that had never been.

He shook his head.

'It was around this time of year that your father died, wasn't it?'

Aaron frowned. Melanie's smile dropped.

'Yes, it was. Why?'

'I'm sorry for your loss. I heard your father was a good man. I never knew mine.'

Aaron looked unsure how to respond. With a shrug, he muttered, 'I suppose. I don't remember him well.'

'Do you remember the night of the accident? You were sleeping in the car, weren't you?'

Aaron's face hardened just a little. 'I was. The jolt woke me.' He reached up and touched the vicious scar down the side of his face. 'A piece of broken glass … I don't remember well.'

'You survived the impact because your car seat got twisted around, didn't it?'

Melanie gave a nervous smile. 'Perhaps we should get back—'

Aaron, however, was staring at Slim. 'I'd forgotten … how did you know that?'

Slim tugged at the collar of his coat to stop the chilly wind getting inside. 'The back window was shattered, and the boot had popped open, I know that from the reports. Did you see anyone? I know that no one saw you.'

Aaron stared at him. 'I was four years old; I can barely remember that night at all … but … I did. I think I saw a man.'

'Who did you see, Aaron? I think I know, but I want you to tell me.'

Aaron stared off into the distance, his eyes narrowing, but he wasn't looking out across the moor, but deep into his past.

'I saw … Brian. Brian Tate.'

Slim nodded. 'He reported the accident. It makes sense that you might have seen him, even if he failed to see you. But I have one last question. What was he doing? What was he doing around the back of the car?'

'He was … my god, I remember now. He was taking something out of the boot. I don't know what it was, but it was big.'

43

SLIM STOOD outside the line of holiday cottages on the road heading east away from Brentor village, a short walk from the entrance to the lane leading down through the valley to Gale Farm.

Set in a dip back from the road, probably to provide a little wind shelter, a battered privet hedge kept them private. From horseback, however, you would have been able to see over the top, into the upper floor windows, even if the hedge had once been a little higher.

Back before they had become holiday cottages, Maggie Leddon had lived in the middle one, commuting from here to Rundlestone County Primary School where she worked as the form teacher to Elissa's class.

Known as a stern, unforgiving woman with an obsession for cleanliness, in the fallout after Elissa's death, she had moved away from the area, most likely to escape the persecution from the locals that Elissa's death had somehow been her fault.

Or so Slim had thought.

It had taken Donald Lane some time to track her

down, mainly because she had moved to London, disappeared into the smoke and eventually remarried.

Slim had been walking back to the car from St. Michael's church when he received the call.

'Slim, it's Don. That lady you asked me to find, I managed to track her down.'

'Maggie Leddon?'

'Yes. It wasn't easy.'

'I appreciate your help, Don. What have you found?'

Donald Lane cleared his throat. 'Well, after moving back to London in 1983 she got married to an accountant called Robert Worthing. It was through trawling the marriages database that I found her, after you told me she was living alone in Devon. If she hadn't got married again, I don't think I'd ever have found her.'

'Is she alive?'

'Sadly not. She died in 1997, but just recently enough that I was able to find an obituary online.'

'How did she die?'

'It didn't say, but she was sixty-two at the time of her death so it could have been a number of things. What it did reveal was that she was survived by a daughter.'

The sickly Leddon girl Linda Gale had mentioned. Slim was almost too stunned to reply. Only after Don asked if he was still on the line was he able to mutter, 'What was her name?'

'Kate Worthing, she was listed as in the obituary, but her age was given as twenty-eight, meaning she would have already been fourteen at the time Maggie got married. I'm guessing Maggie hadn't been married to Kate's father, so Kate took her stepfather's surname.'

'That would make sense. And she would have been twelve or thirteen at the time of Elissa's death? So she could have been living with Maggie in Brentor village?'

'I can't tell you that. What I can tell you is that she had been gravely sick as a child. I managed to find an article written for an online medical journal in 2006 titled *Living with Leukemia*, authored by the aforementioned Kate Worthing. I've sent you a copy. There's a contact email, but I've had no reply. It's possibly out of date. I've been trying to track her since then, but I'm drawing a blank. I can't find her online and it's a fairly common name, so just going by the phone book, so to speak, is going to take a while.'

'Thanks, Don, that's great.'

'Any time I can help, Slim.'

Slim returned to the B&B to read the article. Kate Worthing revealed how she had suffered from leukemia as a child, and had been one of the UK's earliest recipients of a bone marrow transplant in 1977, at the age of eight years old. The cancer had returned at the age of twelve, however, requiring further treatment. She mentioned spending time in Devon in the hope that the cleaner air would help her and that she had been unable to go to school due to the immunodeficiency caused by the disease. The article closed by saying she had been cancer free since 1984, and praised both the NHS and her family for helping her to overcome the illness.

Slim read the article through several times before closing the computer and brewing himself some coffee. The revelations were startling.

Kate would have been living with Maggie Leddon at the time of Elissa's death. Had she been suffering from the early stages of a second bout of leukemia it was possible that her development had been affected, perhaps confusing Elissa, who had thought her of primary school age, and questioned why she didn't attend school. It could also have altered her appearance—maybe she wore a mask, or even a wig to cover little or no hair, or was gaunt and jaundiced.

All of which could make her the girl Philip Reece and maybe Elissa had seen on the moors.

Slim had to track her down. She could provide the key to unlocking the case.

But like Don said, Kate Worthing was a pretty common name. It was the proverbial needle in the haystack, like trying to find a wedding ring dropped somewhere out on the wilds of Dartmoor.

Nevertheless, Slim couldn't help but smile. The investigation, finally, was beginning to crack open.

44

THE NEXT MORNING, he received another email from Kay.

Here's a few more I've figured out. I'm still working through them.

Slim read the list of sentences, most only a few words long. Some were simple, chatty things between friends.

Are you going down to the event on Saturday?

I was almost late. My flask was in my welly!

I caught my jersey on a fence. Dad fixed it.

Are those new shoes?

Others became a little darker:

Did you see her get after Edward in the playground this morning? What a cow.

And then, some directly referenced the girl:

I rode P up the Gale Farm lane to the road yesterday evening. I saw her again. I reckon she's being kept prisoner.

And something else Slim noticed, too. It appeared the conversations were one way, as though the recipient of the messages was answering with a whisper.

You really think so?

No, what if she found out?

It would, wouldn't it?

Bring one, just in case.

The dates on the books were getting worryingly closer to the field trip date. Slim felt sweat prickling his palms as he read the last line in Kay's email.

It's our turn to teach her a lesson.

What had the two girls planned, and how had it gone so wrong that one of them had ended up dead?

Slim wondered if he had enough evidence with which to force a confession. He felt certain he had the answer, but there were just a few pieces still missing.

He called Victoria Aldridge.

'Sorry to bother you yet again.'

'It's quite all right.'

'Did you ever hear Ms. Leddon mention a child?'

'A child?'

'Yes. One of her own.'

Victoria laughed. 'Heavens, no. We all thought of her as this old spinster who'd never been near a man, let alone have a child.'

'Did any of the other girls talk about it? Specifically Elissa and Ginny?'

'Not that I remember. I wasn't in their group when they were together, though. It was pretty much the two of them. We used to say all sorts about Leddon, though. A couple of the boys convinced me she laid eggs.'

Slim smiled. 'And did Elissa have any kind of speech impediment, or a particularly loud voice?'

'No, she was pretty quiet, actually.'

'Oh, right—'

'—but Ginny did, now that I remember. She had something wrong with her jaw that made it click when she spoke. I remember her telling me once how she would need surgery.'

Slim gave a slow nod, then wiped his hands on his jeans. It was almost—but not quite—enough.

'And you said Elissa's horse was called Penelope?'

Victoria shook her head. 'Sorry, Pomegranate. Penelope was Ginny's horse. It's been a long time. I think their horses might have been siblings or something.'

45

IT WAS ENOUGH. Slim packed what he needed into the car and drove over to Brian Tate's house.

The wind was whipping through the few trees as he parked on the road outside Brian's place and climbed out. Dartmoor, wild and tragic, greeted him with its full fury, unleashing a volley of slanting rain as he opened the gate and hurried up the path. At the door he gave a hard knock, cowering beneath the porch as the weather sought him.

'Brian? Ginnette? I need to talk to you.'

The door swung open sharply as though Brian had been standing on the other side. The old hunt master had a grim expression on his face.

'What is it they say about an old dog?' he said. 'Throw him a few scraps....'

'You threw me too many,' Slim said. 'Let me in and tell me the rest.'

'And if I don't?'

'I'll take what I have and go to the police.'

'You have nothing on me. I never hurt Elissa.'

'I know you didn't. But you know more than you said. Both of you do. And I have proof.'

A look of uncertainty passed across Brian's face. 'I could shut this door on you right now—'

'Jake Gale wasn't going back to Brent Tor,' Slim said quickly. 'He was leaving.'

Brian Tate stared at him. The weight of long-hidden secrets hung like a bell jar around his neck. Slim saw him visibly sag.

'I suppose you'd better come in then,' he said at last. 'You utterly relentless bastard.'

Brian grumbled about the kitchen, reluctantly offering Slim a coffee as he sat at the table.

'Ginny should be here for this,' he said. 'Where is she?'

'Can't you leave her alone?'

'No. She's as much a part of this as you are. Perhaps more.'

'She's upstairs.'

'Call her down, please.'

Brian gave Slim a hard stare, then went to the hall and shouted up the stairs. A couple of minutes later Ginny Tate appeared, slinking reluctantly into the kitchen, taking a seat across the table from Slim.

Even though he had briefly spoken to her before, Slim hadn't known her connection to everything, so felt like he was taking a look at her for the first time. She was actually younger than him by a year or so, but while life hadn't been easy for him either, she looked closer to Brian's age. Her face was deeply lined, long, unkempt hair was prematurely greying, and her eyes looked tired and puffy. She dressed as though she rarely left the house, and inactivity had thickened her body. As he faced her, Slim wondered whether he should have come.

'I found your old notebooks,' he said. 'I know about your secret messages to Elissa.'

She looked up, like a reanimated rag doll. 'I burned them years ago….'

'You might have burned yours.'

Ginny looked up at Brian.

'You don't have to listen to this,' he said. 'I can ask him to leave.'

Ginny shook her head. 'No … it's all right.'

'I know it was your plan,' Slim said. 'To prank Maggie Leddon, your teacher. You were angry about her daughter, the little girl you saw in her house. The little girl who didn't go to your school.'

The coffee forgotten, Brian sat down at the table between them.

'Ginny?'

Ginny gave a weak nod. 'He's right,' she said, her voice slow and fragile as though she rarely spoke. 'I told you about her.'

'How did he find out?'

'I have friends who are far cleverer than me,' Slim said. Turning to Ginny, he added, 'You planned to have Maggie Leddon follow you out onto the moor. Tell me the truth. I have my version. Now I want yours.'

'You don't have to say anything,' Brian said, putting a hand over Ginny's wrist.

'I think she does,' Slim said. 'I can see how heavily this has weighed on you, Ginette. You committed no crime. I know that. I just want the truth.'

A single tear trickled down Ginny's cheek.

'We just wanted to get back at her,' she said, so quietly Slim could barely hear. 'She was … tough on us. When I saw she had a daughter, I thought she was … mistreating her.'

'So you planned to lure her out onto the moor?'

'We were only going to scare her, make some noises, then circle back to the coach, pretend we got lost.'

'The knife?'

'Elissa's idea. In case Leddon saw us. In case she … attacked us.'

'Was that very likely?'

Ginny sighed. 'I didn't think so, but Elissa did.'

Slim nodded. 'That makes sense from what I've learned about her. So what happened on the day?'

Ginny sniffed, then wiped away another tear. 'I chickened out.'

'You didn't want to go through with it?'

Ginny shook her head. 'No. So I faked a cold, convinced Dad to let me stay at home that day.'

'But Elissa went through with it anyway.'

Ginny stared at the table as she nodded. 'That's what it looks like.'

'But her plan went wrong.'

Ginny sniffed as she nodded, her eyes filled with tears. Brian shuffled closer and put an arm around her shoulders.

'She was supposed to go back to the coach?'

'Yes. If you arc left through the valley from the tor, you get back to the main road. It's an easy walk.'

'You knew that area well?'

'Yes.'

'So there's no way Elissa got lost.'

Ginny shook her head. 'No.'

'So what happened?'

'I don't know. Something went wrong. She … fell?'

'We both know that's not true, not if Elissa knew the moor as well as you've said, as well as everyone's said.'

Brian started to stand. 'I think you've said enough—'

'Sit, please.'

'You come into my home—'

'Ginny might not know what happened to Elissa, but you do,' Slim said.

'Excuse me?'

'Elissa got spooked that day,' Slim said, speaking fast over Brian's attempt to protest. 'She didn't go back to the coach, but to Gale Farm, where she thought she would be safe. And she ran into Jake Gale.' Slim paused. 'Her real father.'

46

'ARE YOU GENUINELY SERIOUS?' Brian said, staring wide-eyed at Slim. 'You're joking, right?'

'They bear a striking resemblance,' Slim said. 'You couldn't look at the pictures and not see it, and you were his closest friend.'

'It sounds like you're seeing things no one else is,' Brian said.

'Something happened then. I don't know what, but she ended up in the boot of Jake's car. Which is where you later found her.'

Brian gave a dry chuckle. 'You're a fantasist.'

'You were out there that night, waiting for him. He surprised you, though. He wasn't driving back to Brent Tor, but away. He had his son in the back, and his daughter in the boot, tied up or secured in some way. Heaven knows what was going through his mind, but my guess is that he had heard the Lowescrofts were planning to move upcountry and couldn't bear the thought of losing touch with his daughter.'

Brian sighed. 'You got one thing right. He wasn't going back to Brentor. I kicked in some of the skid marks to disguise it.'

'I saw the ones you missed in photographs of the accident scene. No one paid much attention because it made no sense for Jake to be driving away.'

'I don't know where he was going that night, but he was leaving his wife. I know that.'

'Taking his children with him.'

'Child.'

'Children.'

'No, Slim. Child. Only Aaron was in the car.'

'Elissa was in the back. I think she was tied up, but maybe she got her hands free. She tried to get out. There was paint found under her fingernails. It could have come from the boot of a car.'

Brian was slowly shaking his head. He waved a hand through the air like a drunken conductor.

'So tell me what I would have done with her. Come on, enlighten me.'

'The impact killed her, but the coroner missed it, blaming her cause of death on asphyxiation caused by falling unconscious face down in water. By this time, you had heard she was missing. You took her out of the car and you hid her body while you dealt with the police. Later, early the following morning, knowing it would be easier to trace movement by car, you took her back over the moor by horseback, where you laid her down on the grass for the search parties to find. Both horse and cat hair were found on her clothes, in locations consistent with her being lain face down over the front of a horse's saddle. You had a cat at the time, didn't you? It could have come from your clothing. And there was bruising on Elissa's chest consistent with a long, continuous bumping motion.'

Brian was staring at Slim with a look of wonder. Slim felt certain he was about to confess. Beside him, Ginny still stared at the table, her eyes hidden by her hair.

'And why would I have done such a thing?' Brian said. 'Why not just leave Elissa in Jake's car?'

'Because despite what you told me, Jake Gale was your best friend. But even more than that, you admired him, looked up to him. Had his actions been discovered, his reputation and that of his whole family would have been tarnished, and you had it in your power to protect him, to protect them all. It's the same reason you said nothing about what Ginny told you, why you hold your candle vigil every year instead of going to the police. I know you were at the search, because I have pictures of you there. Admit it, Brian. Then everyone can move forward.'

Brian looked for a moment as though he might clap. Instead he just shook his head.

'I can see where your reputation comes from,' he said. 'It's quite some deduction, I must admit. But I can also tell that you have no knowledge of horses. It's ten miles from here to Brent Tor across the moor. Ten miles of off-road terrain, hills, pot holes, marshes. And the weather was terrible that night. We had just one horse at the time that we usually kept here, and I'm pretty sure I can find the records to prove it. A pony, less than thirteen hands, which in layman's terms means not very big. Penelope, she was called. Lovely natured thing. Barely strong enough to carry Ginny at nine, let alone me and a dead girl.' At this Ginny flinched, but Brian just patted her arm and carried on. 'And you think I could have gotten ten miles across Dartmoor, in the dark? You're out of your mind.'

Slim shifted, for the first time fearing a leak in his watertight theory.

'You're a hunt master,' Slim said. 'You're an expert with horses.'

'With my own horse, maybe,' Brian said. 'But the hunt horses are kept elsewhere. Look, Slim, there are aspects of your theory that are ... quaint. But you're way wide of the mark.'

'You took something out of the boot of Jake's car.'

Brian rubbed his nose. 'A hold-all full of clothes. Proof that he was leaving. Other things were inside, too. Ferry tickets from Dover. He was planning to leave the country. I think he knew someone was onto him about what might be going on in his club.' He glanced at Ginny, sitting with her head down. 'My Gin had been right all along. The dead don't talk, but my guess is he'd already heard about Elissa's disappearance, and figured it was a good time to get away. She went to his club, perhaps the police would probe him, witnesses would come forward. I hid the bag until the investigation was over, and a few days later I burned everything.'

'That's all?'

Brian stood up. 'You're right that I wanted to protect Jake's reputation. And after his appalling death, I felt like both he and his family had suffered enough, so I kept my silence. By speaking up, all I was going to do was cause more hurt.' He gave Slim a sideways look. 'Perhaps that's a concept you could learn from. Now, if you don't mind—'

'Stop them,' Ginny said quietly.

'Excuse me?'

Ginny lifted her head just long enough to meet Slim's eyes. He saw in her face a broken woman, and wished he could both take back some of his words, and change the way things were. Sometimes, however, things were just like the stones out on the moor, set, immovable, leaving life no choice but to flow around them.

Then, without another word, Ginny got up and went out into the hall. Slim listened as her footfalls creaked slowly, lethargically, up the stairs.

'She means the bears on Elissa's memorial,' Brian said.

'The bears?'

'The copies of the stupid mascot thing Elissa used to tie to her horse for good luck. Gin rides out there often. It's about all she does outside of the house now. She's always blamed herself, no matter what I say. She finds them … and they upset her.'

'I'll do what I can,' Slim said.

Brian led him to the door, opened it, and stepped back.

'Good luck in your next investigation, Slim,' Brian said. 'And concerning this one, I truly hope this is the last time we'll cross paths.'

Slim could think of nothing to say. He lowered his eyes and walked down the path like a beaten dog. He had reached the gate before he heard the door close behind him.

Out across Dartmoor, the wind had got up, raging across the bridge and hassling the stones where Jake Gale and many others had crashed. Slim stared out at the desolate landscape for a while, as another rage built up within him, an old one, a rage he had never really managed to temper, even through years of struggle.

He was beaten, and his demons would take their revenge if he let them.

He got into the car and drove back across the moor. Fearing what might happen if he went back to the B&B and his room, however, he drove back to Brent Tor, then out along the track onto the moor where he had first followed Andy. He drove right up to where the road ended, stopped the car, and climbed out.

The wind whipped around him, and the rain was

beginning to sheet. Slim took a deep breath, because he had no choice, then tossed the car keys on the ground, in case he never made it back. Then, with his demons at his back, clawing at him, baying for him to turn, turn, *turn* … he walked out onto the moor.

47

Iᴛ ᴡᴀs dark when he made it back to the car some hours later, soaked through, exhausted, his legs cramping, his body shaking. He slumped to the ground by the car and scrabbled in the dirt for his keys.

They were still there. With frozen fingers he picked them up and managed to unlock the car. Inside, out of the wind, he felt a little better, but it was a long time before he could bring himself to drive.

The moor had beaten back his demons for now, but its secrets had beaten him. Humiliated, there was nothing to do but leave this place behind. There would be other cases if he wanted them, other secrets to uncover, if he still had the stomach for the fight.

Part of him, however, thought this might be the end. Where the road had ended for Elissa Lowescroft, it had also ended for John "Slim" Hardy. He had given everything, and he had failed.

Back at the B&B, he stuffed his wet clothes into a plastic bag, took a shower, and then packed away his notes, the photographs he had printed, and all the other miscellany of his failed investigation.

He paid up, then left. He said no goodbyes, offered no last phone calls. He took a road cutting across Dartmoor, heading northeast. He tried not to look out at the wild hills and their ghosts as he drove, but he knew the moor and its mysteries would always haunt him—

Something ran out into the road. He slammed on the brakes, narrowly missing the rabbit as it skittered away into the grass, the sudden lurch of the car throwing his bag into the footwell. As he grabbed it, his notes spewed out, and he groaned, wishing he'd thrown them into the bin at the B&B. He leaned down and gathered them up, trying to ignore the faces of people who now seemed to taunt him.

He couldn't help himself. The demons were still with him, and in a fit of rage that on a deeper level surprised him, he began to claw at the pictures, trying to tear them into pieces. Incapable even of this, he managed only to screw them into a twisted, mangled clump. He made to toss them away, but the bundle caught between the gear stick and the passenger seat.

A face, the same face from two different photographs, several years apart, stared up at him. As Slim stared back, something said by Ginnette Tate caught in his mind and hung there, like a kite, caught in the Dartmoor wind, taunting him with its truth.

Slim gave a little shake of his head. 'It's not....'

He trailed off, slipping the car into reverse and turning the car back around, the final word left hanging like a forgotten breath.

...impossible....

48

Slim signed in as a guest, introducing himself as Mike Lewis, BBC researcher. The lie was enough to get him past the staff, the A4 sheet with his stated research aims, together with a fake company logo enough to get an audience with the old man in Room 27. As Slim knocked gently on the open door, the white-haired man in a wheelchair waved for him to sit down. They left the room door open, but to Slim's relief, there were no other people within earshot.

'Thank you for allowing me to see you,' Slim said, reaching out to take the old man's hand and then introducing himself. There was a little strength left in the grip, which pleased Slim. He had no choice but to be here, but he wanted to lay down his cards as gently as possible.

'Yes, well, apart from the children, I don't get a lot of visitors these days.'

His voice, the brightness in his eyes, told Slim his faculties were all there. He had got lucky at last.

'The first thing I'd like you to do is take a look at a picture for me,' Slim said, trying to keep his voice level, to quell the excitement that he was finally about to cross the line. 'I took it yesterday afternoon and printed it out at the post office up the road.'

He pulled a plastic file out of his rucksack and slid out a large glossy photograph.'

The man leaned forwards, then reached up and nudged the glasses up his nose with one arthritic hand. He frowned for a moment, then nodded. 'Oh, you went up to the yard, did you? I didn't think anyone would have any interest in that old girl.'

'I do,' Slim said, tilting the photograph that he had taken, to look at the contents one more time. Sometimes, what was in plain view was the most difficult to see, the easiest to ignore. Like the old coach, rusting away in the corner of the yard, weed strewn, its doors and windows long gone, many of its parts stripped away, its crusty, flaking seats and aisle piled with other unwanted junk.

James Greg leaned back. 'She was a good runner,' he said. 'Served us well for twenty-odd years.'

'But most memorable for one day in particular,' Slim said. 'Let me show you one more picture.'

This was the moment he was dreading. He pulled out the second file from his bag, but before he'd even lifted it up, James's face changed, realisation dawning. As Slim held out the picture of Elissa Lowescroft, the old man's eyes filled with tears. The elation that Slim felt at knowing he had finally got it right was tempered by the heartbreaking look in the old man's face.

'Oh dear,' he said. 'Not her. Not poor Elissa.'

'I know what happened that day,' Slim said. 'But I'd like to hear it in your words. She came back to the coach, didn't she?'

James reached up a shaking finger and wiped a tear off his cheek.

'That poor girl … oh, that poor girl.'

'Please, James.'

'Am I in trouble? I suppose I deserve it.'

'I'm not the police. I'm just a … researcher. I just want to know what happened. The truth.'

James ran a hand through what was left of his hair. 'I planned to take this to the grave, but I suppose … she … Elissa … she … she must of come back. I had no idea. I was wandering about, waiting for the kids to come back down the hill. We were due to leave at three and I remember it was ten to. Old Gale brought a herd through.'

'A herd?'

'Cattle. They came down that road from Gale Farm, and started misbehaving in the car park. I got back on the coach and shut the door. A few bumped against the side, the buggers. Thought to myself I wish someone would have a word with Gale about that, but you know farmers, they make their own rules.'

Slim smiled. 'I've come to that conclusion myself.'

'One of those bumps must of been her, opening the luggage locker and getting in. I remember it wasn't quite closed, figured I'd forgotten to shut it properly. Lock had broke, hadn't got around to getting it fixed.'

'She was in the luggage locker under the coach?'

'Didn't know it then. Still don't know why. The others came back, panicking that a lass was lost up there. I offered to go up and have a look about, but the headmaster told me to go down the road to a phone box and call the police.'

'What happened after that?'

'When I got back, the kids had loaded up their stuff, bags of twigs and rocks they'd picked up on the moor, for some art thing they were planning, I suppose. After a bit of craziness with that young lad, after the police showed up, I took the kids back to the school, then drove back to the yard.'

'Elissa was still in the luggage locker?'

James sighed. 'Must of been.'

'And you didn't know?'

'No idea. Emptied the bags out at the school, didn't see her. Wasn't 'til early the next morning that I was out cleaning, noticed one of them panels at the back looked loose.'

James lowered his head, reached up and pinched his nose. For a few minutes Slim waited while the old man cried.

'She'd … she'd somehow got in through that there paneling, right in to where all the mechanics are, and she must of got stuck. We weren't the cleanest back in them days, engine fumes must of done for her. I got her out but she was … she was cold.'

'What did you do?'

'I tried to call, I swear I did. But by then I'd heard about her disappearance on the radio, as well as Jake Gale's crash out at Postbridge. I guess they had no one left for the phones. I figured there might be a search, so I drove straight up there, thinking I'd let them know, hand her over. It was still early, not yet light. When I got there, though, that's when I had … me moment.'

'Your moment?'

The old man sniffed. 'Me moment of madness. No one was about, see. They were all out on the hill. I thought what it might do to the kids. My boys were both in the same school, one a year above, one below. And the business, it was only three of us at the time. The damage to our reputation would have ruined us. So I took her up there, up the way they'd gone, and I laid her down on the grass. I put her … I put her face down, because I couldn't bear … couldn't bear to look at her eyes. Then I wandered up the hill a bit and tagged on with one of the searching crews.'

Slim sat back and gave a slow nod. 'Thank you,' he said.

'Am I in trouble? I know what I did was wrong, and I know I deserve to be punished. But I didn't kill her. I had no idea she was even in there, and I still don't know why.'

'My understanding is that it was a practical joke gone wrong,' Slim said. 'But the main thing is that you've told me the truth.'

'I'll tell the police if you want.' The old man sniffed. 'I'll tell them everything.'

'I don't think that's necessary, but I think there is one person who might want to know.'

'Who?'

Slim shifted on his seat to look back through the open doorway. 'You can come in now.'

There was the scrape of a chair on carpet, then a figure appeared in the doorway. Robina Lowescroft stood there, eyes filled with tears.

'Oh, James,' she said. 'Why didn't you ever say?'

'Robina … Robina … I'm so sorry.'

Slim stood up, turning away just enough to wipe a tear from his own eye. 'I'll give you two some privacy,' he said. 'I'll go and see if there's a coffee machine down the hall.'

49

FINDING the old coach in the corner of the yard at Greg's Coaches had been a bonus. Aware he was looking at a possible crime scene, Slim had been careful as he looked inside, but when he returned for a second look, he had seen where the paneling of the inside luggage locker could have come away, revealing a space in among the engine parts where a thin, athletic girl might have been able to squeeze. It was Slim's guess that she had been knocked unconscious, perhaps dying later of asphyxiation back at the coachyard.

While he was unsure whether paint scraped from the coach's engine area could be matched with what had been found under Elissa's nails so long after the event, Slim had come across another possible piece of evidence linking James Greg to the events.

The reverend had finally got back to him with the old log book for St. Michael's church dating from 1982. Five days after the events, someone had written "Lord, please forgive me".

Under the guise of Mike Lewis in his role as a

historical researcher for the BBC, Slim had secured some old ledgers from James Greg's son, who now ran Greg's Coaches. Kay had confirmed the handwriting matched.

While none of his evidence would be enough in a court of law, it had been enough to give him the confidence to approach the eighty-eight-year-old James Greg. Another stroke of luck had been that the old man had both possessed the faculties to talk and been willing to confess. Slim had seen the good in the man, had understood that he had been the victim of misfortune, and had made a poor choice. He had left the final decision up to Robina, but could see in James's eyes that carrying the secret for so long had been punishment enough.

Later, over coffee in a Tavistock café, Robina told him what had happened.

'I said that I forgave him,' she said. 'He was always such a nice man. He did the school run for years. I remember that afterwards he seemed a little sheepish around me, distant. I thought it was just out of pity, like he didn't know what to say. At least now I know the truth.'

'Will you tell anyone?'

'Maybe Brenda, when I'm ready. It's been so long. I'll probably wait for James to pass, spare him any more hurt.'

'You know, I got a lot of things wrong,' Slim said. 'Badly, unforgivably wrong. I thought Elissa was Jake Gale's illegitimate daughter, and I made assumptions based on that fact.'

Robina let out a chuckle. 'No, she was ours. Jake was a player, and I'm afraid so was I, but she was definitely Gordon's. She was the spitting image of his mother.' She shrugged. 'Jake and me … can I just blame it on the seventies?'

'You can do as you wish. There are few of us without

skeletons. I have a whole closet of my own that I struggle to keep closed.'

'Well, you have my thanks, Slim. I'm not sure that I feel much happier about things, but at least I have some closure. Sometimes that's enough.'

'I'm glad I helped in some way.'

'You did. I'm still struggling to come to terms with the truth, but I feel better for it. What will you do now?'

Slim thought about the next person he needed to visit, and glanced up at a clock on the wall behind the counter.

'I have one or two more things to do, then I think I'll head back upcountry for a while.'

'Whatever you choose to do next, I wish you well.'

50

IT HAD TAKEN a bit of deduction, but he had found her in the end. Four people on the list Audrey had given him had variants on the name "Kate", and he had finally discovered that a volunteer counselor called Catherine Reilly had once gone under the name of Kate Worthing.

'I'm two husbands deep,' said the spritely woman in her mid-fifties as she hiked alongside Slim to the top of Brent Tor. They had picked a warm and clear late November day, but there was still a glistening sheen of frost visible in the valleys and the shady places behind rocks.

'I was sick right through childhood,' she told him, setting a pace that Slim struggled to match. 'A lot of it is a blur, to be quite honest. Treatment programmes, hospitals, so much pain. I know Mum brought me down here in the hope the clean air would help, but it wasn't long before we had to go back to London. For months at a time my immune system was vulnerable, meaning I had to wear a mask and gloves all the time, even around the house, which I hated. I wasn't allowed to go to school. It used to drive me crazy.'

'It was you on the moors that day, wasn't it?'

Catherine sighed. 'Mum had mentioned a school trip. I loved walking on the moors, but she used to call between classes to check up on me, make sure I was still at home. When I knew she'd be unable to get to the phone, I couldn't help going out onto the moor to have a look. I had my hat and mask on, just in case I ran into her, but I'd only got as far as the stream when the fog rolled in, so I started heading back. And then a man came running out of nowhere. He took one look at me and started screaming. It scared the hell out of me, so I ran off, back to the house.'

'You didn't hear what happened?'

'My mother told me nothing. Not a thing. She was trying to protect me, I know that now. I didn't even know a girl had died until I came back here ten years ago, but one day I was out walking on the moor and came across her memorial.'

'Did you remember her?'

'I looked her up, found a couple of pictures. That's what led to the bear thing.'

'With Andy?'

'Yes. I was out with a group of patients one day, working as a guide. We walked past the memorial, and I mentioned how her favourite toy had been a little blue bear, and wondered if she was missing it. As a craft project back at the disability centre we made some toys. Andy Johnson made a blue bear. I suggested Elissa would like it. I didn't know his OCD was so bad that he would make them over and over again.'

'Someone kept taking them away,' Slim said. 'I found by putting a microphone in one that it was Ginny Tate. She's still suffering from her own trauma related to the event.'

'I got in touch with her,' Catherine said. 'I think that if

she knows who I am and what part I played in things, she'll have a better chance of coming to terms with it. And she might let the bears rest.'

'Along with Elissa, and Andy, and everyone else involved,' Slim said.

'How about you?' Catherine said glancing at him as he struggled to keep up.

'I could really do with a rest,' Slim said with a tired sigh. 'How about we stop on that rock over there for a quick cup of coffee?'

51

AUDREY JOHNSON DIDN'T LOOK CONVINCED. 'The bear was Elissa's lucky toy,' Slim told her. 'Andy learned that from … an old acquaintance of Elissa. Sadly, another person was taking them away, restitching the mouths, putting them back. I've spoken to Elissa's mother, and they're planning to add a permanent stone one to the memorial. Perhaps Andy could be there for the ceremony? I think after that, he can rest.'

Audrey nodded. 'It's not the answer I was expecting, but it's something,' she said. 'I thank you for your efforts.'

Slim smiled. 'All my best to Andy,' he said. 'I think he's lucky to have a mother like yourself.'

'Thank you for saying that, Mr. Hardy.'

Slim nodded, then took his leave.

He met Simon Clifford in their regular Tavistock café. Through the window, a group of ducks waddled along the edge of the river.

'I came to the end of the road,' Slim said. 'I had a number of theories, but they all came to nothing in the end. I overturned every stone I could find, but sometimes a man has to admit defeat.'

Simon gave a disappointed nod. 'So, you don't think we'll ever know what truly happened to Elissa Lowescroft that night on the moor?'

Slim looked up, meeting Simon's eyes. He held the old reporter's gaze for a moment, then said quietly, 'No, I'm afraid not.'

Outside, the café sign rattled as though to acknowledge his dishonesty, caught in a sudden gust of wind that could have come down from the wild hills of Dartmoor.

Slim stood up, shook Simon's hand, and excused himself. The road was calling, and he was keen to leave this part of England, and its secrets, behind.

END

ABOUT THE AUTHOR

Jack Benton is a pen name of Chris Ward, the author of the dystopian *Tube Riders* series, the horror/science fiction *Tales of Crow* series, and the *Endinfinium* YA fantasy series. He also writes seasonal romance as CP Ward, as well as a few other things.

Here the Road Ends is the ninth mystery to feature John "Slim" Hardy. There will be more…

Chris would love to hear from you:
www.amillionmilesfromanywhere.net/tokyolost
chrisward@amillionmilesfromanywhere.net

ACKNOWLEDGMENTS

Many thanks as always go to those who helped with this book. Jenny Avery for her incredible knowledge and eye for detail. You really saved this one! Thanks also to Elizabeth Mackey for the cover, and Paige Sayer for proofreading. And as always, to my muses, Jenny Twist and John Dalton.

Finally, for those of you who support me via Patreon, thanks very much. In no special order: Donna Askins, Mike Wright, Rosemary Kenny, Jane Ornelas, Ron, Gail Beth Le Vine, Jennie Brown, Janet Hodgson, Karen P, Paul Go, Sharon Kenneson, and Dr. Kat Crispin.

And for everyone who's Bought me a Coffee recently: Norma, Library Anne, Sarah House, Paula, Venita Garnett, Matt Korbich, Sonia Finch, Joann Davis, Allen from the US, Donna Askins, Vicky B, Sherie Williams Ellen, I.M. Hanson, Randall Balsmeyer, Peter Jaspers-Fayer, Sam Cleve, Carol Nash, Patsy Mcclure, Brinda Arnold, Grey Cynic, Monica Demmerle, Donald McLellan, Amy Thay, Cesar Sandoval, Ann Chesterton, Nova Kay, Someone, Jennie B, Mary, Richard Herndon, Claire, Ian Yates-Laughton, Jim Naughton, Rowan

Anderson, Andrea Richards, Malcolm from Canada, Elizabeth M. Dykes, Rachel G, Keith Turner, Sheri Bellefeuille, Niall Nicolson, Amelie Eva, Paul M, Laurie Jones, and Aileen MacKinnon. Thank you. Your support means so much.

Last and not least, to all my readers. Thank you for supporting my books and I look forward to bringing you the next John "Slim" Hardy adventure.

JB

February 2024